MAGICAL MURDER MYSTERY TOUR

TIMOTHY W. AYERS

This is a work of fiction. Names, characters, places, and incidents are products of the author's imagination or are used fictitiously and are not to be construed as real. Any resemblance to actual events, locations, organizations, or persons, living or dead, is entirely coincidental.

World Castle Publishing, LLC
Pensacola, Florida
Copyright © Timothy W. Ayers 2019
Paperback ISBN: 9781950890163
eBook ISBN: 9781950890170
First Edition World Castle Publishing, LLC, June 24, 2019
http://www.worldcastlepublishing.com

Licensing Notes

Cover: Karen Fuller
Editor: Maxine Bringenberg

DEDICATIONS AND RECOGNITION

This book is dedicated to Ringo Starr, Paul McCartney, and the memories of John Lennon and George Harrison. Their music was the soundtrack to my early years and the underpinnings of this book. It is also dedicated to the memory of Sam Moses, who was a great friend. His early passing gave me the kick in the pants that I needed. Life is too short, so accomplish all that you can.

I have to begin my thanks with a big one to my big brother, Jack the cop, for fact checking as I wrote each chapter and for the constant encouragement that this book was my best. Family is important to me, and I want to thank them all for the ways they encouraged me. As you read the book, you will see parts of you in the different characters. To my Dillard's family I give a nod of appreciation, since many of them were the models for some of the minor characters in the book. Thanks also to my old high school rock 'n' roll band who, in this book, became the Moondogs.

Finally, a big thanks to Jody, a fellow artist, writer, and Beatles fan. It was her, after reading my first few chapters for NANOWRIMO, that claimed *Magical Murder Mystery Tour* was a for sure best seller. She has read the book in every stage and encouraged me to get it done.

CHAPTER 1

"Blue jays are nasty birds," he mumbled to himself as he carefully and gently placed the bloody, severed head back on her body as if he were an artist creating an installation piece at the Figge Museum. In his mind, in some twisted recess, he was an artist — an artist of the macabre, an artist of death, an artist of revenge, a conceptual artist creating his first installation piece to elicit fear and befuddlement.

"Blue jays would pick your pretty little face clean if I left you here, my dearest, but I care too much for that to happen." The macabre artist paused and pulled a deep breath of air through his nostrils. He smiled. "Why anyone would think Blue Jay Way was a good name for a nice street in a gentrifying part of town totally befuddles me. What do you think, sweetie? No answer?" He giggled as he continued his precise head placement on the torso. He stood back and framed her body with his two thumbs touching and palms up, facing her. "That's okay. I don't like my dates very talkative anyway."

He sat next to her, rubbing his long, latex clad fingers through his thinning, graying strands of hair, and breathed out a long, satisfied sigh. "You may not thank me now, but someday you will. For you, my dear," he softly purred as he glanced over towards her as if she were his evening date, "are the first of my.... I hopefully say," his eyes rose to the lightening sky, "that you are my first of my many odes to all things Beatles." He rested his head back, then glanced at his gold watch. "Oh, you are right, I'd better finish my work of art and get on my way. You have such an eye for good visuals. I am so glad that I met you at that café near the art museum. You have been the most perfect model."

He stood and reached into his backpack, pulling out a pair of round framed sunglasses. He lovingly placed them over her ears, dropping her long, black Asian hair down along her shoulders. Satisfied, the madman next snatched a fresh grapefruit from the bag, wrapped the lifeless fingers of one hand around it, and softly posed it in her motionless lap. He drizzled fake snow on the ground next to her, and placed the other hand palm down in the dusting of shredded plastic.

He smiled. It was a satisfied smile, a happy smile. His masterpiece was finished. He stood erect, filled with an internal glee that emanated from his eyes. He blew her a kiss and bowed with his left arm swinging dramatically through the air before removing his rubber gloves. He placed them in a disposable bag that he would discard miles away from the location on Blue Jay Way. His last act was to take a few photos of his work of art. Not so much as a remembrance, but primarily for his press kit. He giggled again at that thought: a serial killer with his own press kit. Maybe he should hire a public relations spokesperson. Whom? He mused over a volume of famous names. He giggled once more at his own thought.

The sun's rays were breaking over the buildings, cutting the foggy mist with bands of yellow, red, and orange as he walked with the click of his Cuban heels echoing off the awakening street. He had to make a phone call, and knew just the place to make it. He rocked back and forth, from side to side in a private dance to music that was drumming a rhythm and a rock 'n' roll beat in his mind. Two blocks later he found a rare pay phone and put on new latex gloves. He dialed a number and waited for the prompt to punch in the extension code, then pushed the button on his MP3 player. He smiled and swayed like a 1920s jazz singer to the rhythm of the Beatles' "Blue Jay Way." He stopped the recording and hung up the phone. In a few hours, someone would hear the song and another someone would find the body. Then the glorious game would begin.

How long before John "Moondog" Watson would figure out he was in the midst of the case of his life, he thought? Yes, soon they would be matching wits against one another. Soon. The killer gave a twisted smile as his eyes danced with a sparkling happiness. He had waited a long time for this day. A long time for this all to begin. All the planning he had done, and of course, he had spent his immense fortune on this lifelong dream of revenge. His heels clicked as he half strolled and half danced down the street, singing, "It's been a hard day's night, and I've been killing like a dog...."

CHAPTER 2

John Watson walked into the police station a little slower than he had done over thirty years ago when he started on the force. The pace was slower and the heart was a lot lighter. He was one month from retirement. He had already bought a small, retail building in an upcoming, hipster neighborhood along the Mississippi River called East Davenport. His dream to have a Beatles memorabilia and record shop was coming to fruition. Abby Road had opened the week before, the grand opening was this upcoming weekend, and his picture was splashed all over the Lifestyle section of the Sunday paper and the River City Reader. He smelled success and the faint scent of stress leaving his body. Success because the Beatles were still as popular as ever, with more and more hipster teens and millennials rediscovering their music. The stress reduction would come after he was done chasing the bottom dwellers and river rats through the cesspools and sewers of his lifelong home. Moondog was the head detective. He drew every piece of shit and sludge case the department had to offer. If it wasn't for the good things in his life, like his band and his new shop, John would have lost his faith in humanity altogether.

After over twenty-five years as a homicide detective, Watson had seen the very worst of people in his multiple cities. The only thing that had kept his attitude up and his mind alive was his dream of opening Abbey Road. John

"Moondog" Watson had been collecting Beatles trinkets, records, posters, and pictures since he was thirteen years old. Forty-one years later, he was ready to sell them all for a severe profit.

Since he was sixteen John had played in a Beatles tribute band called Johnny and the Moondogs. It was a name the Beatles had discarded, but Watson felt it was appropriate to use it. The Moondog name eventually drifted over to him. The officers at the station called him Moondog. The public knew him as Moondog. Only his ex-wife called him Johnny, and his only daughter affectionately called him Moondaddy.

"Hey, Moondog, only a month to go. Are you going to make it, old man?" his partner, Sammy Moses, joked as he tossed a wadded-up paper at him. Sammy was a lot younger than Moondog, but had shown tremendous ability. His dark good looks and thin mustache gave him a swarthy, dangerous look that drew women and informants to him. They had been teamed with the thought that the old man could pass down all he knew about murder investigations before he retired. Sammy learned quick, never second guessed, and turned into a rising star on the force. Moondog was proud of him. Sammy was his legacy, and it would be a good legacy.

"I'll make it as long you don't drag us into some crossfire, Moses. Besides, I believe I start a month long, desk duty assignment. Who did they team you up with?" Moondog asked as he dropped his sport coat over the back of an antique, splintering wooden chair.

"I was hoping for Jennifer Lopez, but I got her distant cousin, Jerry Lopez. Not as pretty, and he certainly can't dance, but he does have a nice booty," Moses fired back with a smile that curled the left side of his mouth while he reached around and slapped Lopez's ass.

"Jerry is a good cop. You two will do fine together. Now, I better get to my easy, cushy, non-violent desk work," Moondog said as he noticed the light blinking on his phone extension. He picked up the receiver and dialed the code to retrieve the call.

Moondog recognized the song right away as the eerie, sitar influenced sound of "Blue Jay Way" came through the phone earpiece. He knew the lyrics.

"Okay, who's the joker who put the Beatles song on my message machine?" Moondog said with a laugh as he raised his head and extended both arms upward and outward towards his friends of three decades.

"What song was it?" Moses asked without raising his head from the paperwork that surrounded him.

"'Blue Jay Way.' Is this some kind of trivia question?" He asked while staring from cop to cop.

"What did you say?" asked the captain as he walked out of his office. Roudebush was always in a bad mood and terse. He was miserable. His home life was miserable, and his job made him even more miserable.

"I said someone put a song in my voicemail box as a joke," the detective answered.

"What song did you say it was, Moonie?" the captain pointedly spat out.

"'Blue Jay Way.'"

"It may be a coincidence, but some old fart out walking his dog early this morning discovered a dead body sitting like she was sleeping, and it's on Blue Jay Way," the captain said as he rubbed his hand over his bald head. "Your desk duty will have to wait. I want you on this case, Moondog. Take Moses and Lopez with you. The investigation team is probably already there."

The captain handed Moondog the location and went back to his office. Watson smiled. He really didn't want to be inside in a safe office. He would miss the street, and maybe this case would be right up his alley — or better yet, right up his Blue Jay Way.

CHAPTER 3

Watson pushed the passenger's side door open with a distinctive "I need greased" creak. He wouldn't miss that, he thought. He moved towards the crime scene with his eyes pulling in everything they scanned. Moondog was an exceptional cop and a superior detective. His eye was trained. He knew that the solution to any mystery was in the details found and properly reassembled. Solving a crime was like putting together a jigsaw puzzle, he would tell Moses. First you turn all the pieces over, find the frame, then fill in the picture. It was never easy, but it also never varied. Stick to the process and you solve crimes, Moondog would say.

Blue Jay Way was one of the last remaining brick streets in the city. The locals had fought to keep it that way. None of them wanted to see asphalt plastered over their distinctively old bricks. It had pits and pitches, but the bricks gave the community an older, more genteel feeling. The bricks also gave a detective grooves and recesses where unseen clues could hide. Moondog turned to Moses and said, "I want them to check every brick for blood. I also saw a phone booth back about two blocks. I am betting my phone call came from there. I want it dusted for prints and the phone records of calls from that phone for the last two months. If he used it then he knew it worked. The only way to know it works is to try it. I want to know who he called and why."

As he approached the scene, Moondog paused. The

coroner and criminal investigation team had been there for twenty minutes. The photographer was stowing his camera to leave the scene when Watson tapped him on the shoulder. "Not so fast, George, I want you to take more shots," the detective said. Old George Patterson was a year or so away from retirement himself. In recent months he had taken to cutting corners and doing a less than stellar job. He would get the old George back, because he knew he needed it after his first glance over the scene.

"Got them from all angles, Moondog. Hey, I thought you were retiring," George stated as he continued to pack his camera.

"Not yet, but I want more pictures. I want every angle." Moondog waved his arms over the entire scene, along the brick street and even into the sky. "I want every detail recorded. I want pictures of the spot where the body is sitting after they remove it. I want shots of every house within seeing distance. I want the street photographed. If a friggin' bird flies by, I want a picture of it. I want everything, and I want it before I retire, old buddy," Watson commanded. He leaned heavily on the old buddy part, since they were truly old friends. Patterson would do it because Watson reminded him of how George used to do his job, and because they'd come up through the Quad Cities school system together, then both landed at the department. A few times, when George was the target of class bullies, John's big frame and slightly older age had put a damper on any attack.

"Moondog, you're the boss, but can you tell me why?" George asked. He pulled his camera from the bag and fished out the lenses he would need.

"We have a serial killer in the making, and I want to stop him ASAP," Moondog stated. The heads of every man and woman within earshot snapped in his direction at the sound of the words "serial killer."

"One killing is not a serial killer, old man," snickered Jerry Lopez, the young detective. Moses shot him a glance as a distinct sign that he should shut up. Lopez realized his error and added, "Sorry, Detective, that was out of line. I am here to learn. Tell us why you think it is a serial killer when it is only one murder."

"Lopez, someday you will be a good detective, but you have to learn to trust your gut. When I say that I don't mean my gut feeling is an intuition, I mean, it is a lifetime collection and mixture of knowledge that rolls around inside my brain. The brain pulls together details faster than you think. What comes out of my brain's processing is my gut feeling. Let me take you to school, and Moses, you can write it all down.

"First of all, the phone call told us where to find the body. It was a Beatles song. Our victim was obviously killed elsewhere, blood drained, and then moved here. She was not laid here to hide her, but placed here in a certain position, her head placed back on her torso and sunglasses added. What you see is a word picture." Watson's long strides took him closer to the murdered woman, with Lopez and Moses on his heels. "The whole crime scene has been set like piece of art. It says something, and we, as cops, are to decipher what the killer is trying to say. Once we figure that out, we can form a profile of the killer. This is an invitation to a game, Lopez. A game means there will be more pieces to the puzzle, and more pieces mean a serial killer." When Watson concluded his lesson he turned and grabbed Lopez by the shoulder, leaning in and lifting off his sunglasses so the younger detective could see his eyes.

"What does it say, then? Why the grapefruit and the fake

snow?" timidly asked Lopez, feeling more like a first day rookie than a five-year veteran.

"The killer does not want me to retire. This message is for me. He knows that I'm the only cop in town that will figure it out. It is a bold, well scripted challenge to me. He knows Beatles history, and he has an opinion about it. The woman is Asian." Moondog gestured to the sitting corpse. "She is posed to reflect photographs of Yoko Ono." Moonie leaned forward and pointed to the fruit in her hand. "The grapefruit would confuse most people, but...," he jabbed a finger into the air, "*Grapefruit* was the name of her first book. Her severed head was not what killed her. That was done later, and it is a message. It is a commentary." Watson leaned on the hood of a black and white. "Our killer blames Yoko for breaking up the Beatles by removing the head, John Lennon. He chose Blue Jay Way as the location for two reasons: it was an easy clue, and because George Harrison and Lennon were the closest of the Beatles."

"What about the snow, Moonie?" Moses asked.

"There is something in the back of my head, but I can't put my finger on it. That's what the picture says, but all of that won't tell us who the killer is. That is in the details of the crime scene."

Watson slipped from Beatles historian back to his hard-boiled detective mode with a sweep of his hand. "He left something behind. He missed something. I want to find that something. Or he left something behind that he wanted left behind. He is out to get me, and he wants me to know why. At this point, I don't know why. That is my mystery to solve." Watson rose from the hood of the police cruiser. "We're done here. Sammy, drop me off at my store and then build the board for me at the office. I want every detail possible on it."

15

Watson headed towards the car to allow the crime scene team to finish their work. Moses and Lopez moved quickly behind him. The sun grew stronger, burning the mist out of the air. Moondog reached for his round, wire-rimmed sunglasses in his coat pocket and settled them back on his face. He quickened his pace. There was something nagging at the back of his brain—something he needed to get from his head to the stack of clues he was building, but it eluded him.

Three steps from the car, his phone rang.

"Watson here," he answered.

The other end of the line yielded only a song. "Ain't She Sweet" drifted out of his phone, one of the Beatles' first recordings, and had been the flip side of "My Bonnie," recorded by Tony Sheridan on lead vocals and the Fab Four backing him up. Then the line went dead.

Watson knew the killer had eyes on them. He stopped to look around. From somewhere near them, the killer watched with a sense of satisfaction and insane glee. This case would be the challenge of his life.

He shut off his phone and climbed back in the car. He turned his face to the window and whispered, "Welcome to my world, wack-job. I will catch you, you insane bastard."

CHAPTER 4

Moondog unlocked the front door of his Beatles memorabilia shop, Abby Road. He didn't turn on the lights or change the sign from closed to open. He needed time to think, to solve the riddle. The hand in the snow meant something, but he didn't know what.

Watson turned on his computer and went to the Wikipedia page on Yoko Ono. He scanned the information, looking for it. He found the answer. Yoko's first child was named Kyoko, and one of Yoko's more popular tunes, if one could term any of her music as popular, was entitled, "Don't Worry Kyoko (Mummy's Only Looking for Her Hand In the Snow)." Was it a clue, or just part of an elaborate work of art in murder?

Moondog pushed himself away from the computer and walked to his book selection. There were autographed copies of their biographies, *Spaniard In the Works* by Lennon and six copies of Yoko's book, *Grapefruit*. He grabbed the first copy and thumbed through it. Then the second. He had a hunch. Then the third. As he cracked open the fourth copy, the book fell open to a note created with words and letters cut by a razor from an old yellowed magazine. It was a simple note. "Answer your phone."

Just then the business land line rang. Watson hurried to it and snatched the receiver from the cradle. The music started.

"Hey, Bungalow Bill

What did you kill, Bungalow Bill?"

The repeated verse played again and again until the song ended. Moondog slouched down in his chair. "Now, I have a name for you, you bastard." He let the name out slowly. "Bungalow Bill, the game is on." He said it aloud while raising his eyes to a recently installed camera. Could Bungalow Bill hear him or see him? Most likely he had hacked into the sophisticated surveillance system that John had installed in the store.

Watson picked up his phone and dialed the police station. "Sammy, come get me," was all he said. Once Moses had picked up Moondog from the store, he asked his partner to head to a local coffee shop that he had never patronized before. He wanted the conversation to be private, and at this point he felt that nowhere he frequented would be private. The killer had been setting things up for a long time. Too many coincidences meant there were no coincidences at all. The killing was not a random act. It was methodical, premeditated, and had all the elements of a work of art. A demented, sick, and violent work of art.

Once in a booth at the back of the coffee shop, Moondog gave a detailed account of what had happened at Abby Road. "That is pretty bizarre, Moonie. How did he know you would open the book then? He has to have some kind of surveillance inside your place."

Moses rubbed his eyes as if he could not believe the recent turn of events. The younger cop looked up at the stress lines forming on his mentor's face, and knew the wheels inside the old guy's mind were turning fast.

"I used your cousin to set up the cameras and recording equipment at the store. Meet him privately and ask for all the names of people on his crew, where he bought the equipment, and the software. It was hacked, for sure. Lean on him hard if you have to," Watson told him as he took another sip of his black coffee. "There is no doubt about it, but I didn't have it connected to the Internet. It had to be breached when it was installed or at a later point, then connected to the outside somehow." John sipped at his coffee. "Have him drop by Abby Road and go over the system with a fine-toothed comb. Bungalow Bill is going to expect me to do it, so this won't throw him off his game. He seems to know my investigative routine as well as you do, or even better." He took another sip and stared up over his round wire-rimmed reading glasses. "While you're at it, look into other detectives that we worked with. See if any of them talked to someone about me or about my methods. Bungalow Bill is going to kill again soon, or he already has and we just don't know about it yet.

"Also, check into Lopez. I don't think he's connected, but it wouldn't hurt to make sure. Somebody knows a lot about me and a lot about the Beatles. This is a vendetta against me, and the bastard is going to find out that I never lose a fight. Got it?" Moondog said with a cold stare in his eyes. He couldn't retire as long as this killer was loose.

"Are you going to postpone your opening this Saturday?" Sam asked as he lifted his glass of iced tea to his lips.

"Nope. Bungalow Bill will be there in some form, whether it is a proxy or himself. He will be there."

The rest of his comments were interrupted by a phone call to Moses from the captain.

"Get your ass and Watson's back here, now. I want some answers. Find out who leaked the crime scene photos to the press. It is all over the morning newspapers," the captain screamed into the phone.

Moondog tossed a few dollars on the table to cover the tab, slid quickly across the seat, and was out the door. He remembered seeing a Quad Cities Times paper box outside the restaurant. He dropped in some change and grabbed a copy. The front page headline was TERRORIST LOOSE IN CITY. Below it were several pictures of the crime scene. He read the first few lines to Moses as he moved up next to him.

"A woman found beheaded in a downtown, residential community. The local police captain, Harry Roudebush, was called but would not comment on an ongoing investigation. An unidentified source stated that it looked like a terrorist is loose in the city. This follows the beheadings and attacks that have occurred around the country and in Canada."

"Who writes this bullshit?" Moses quipped, jabbing his finger into the newspaper.

"People without a clue. I'm starting to think we are close to joining them in the without a clue department. We need a lead in this investigation, and so far all I have are questions. Let's go back and see what the crime scene boys pulled from the area, and try to add up what we have," Moondog said.

CHAPTER 5

There was a violent storm rolling in at the police station. Captain Roudebush was yelling, banging papers, and pushing his crime scene photographer hard, verbally and physically, to confess to leaking the photos. Watson waded into the middle of the scene and tossed the paper down in front of the captain.

"This photo was taken hours before we got to the scene. You can still see the wisps of fog in the background, and the lighting was very dim. You need to get someone down to the newspaper and get their photos. Also see what else the killer sent them." Watson held the paper up in front of the captain's eyes. "I remember the mist was almost gone when I got there, and was completely gone moments after I left. It wasn't our people who leaked it." Moondog moved to the rear of where the photographer sat, and placed his big hands on the man's shoulders. "Patterson is too good at his job to screw up like that. It was the killer doing his own press release." Watson paused while moving to Patterson's side. "He also did us a favor. He put the press on a terrorist trail while we know it is serial killer. This guy is going to make us look like fools if we don't get out in front of this quickly. Trust me, Captain, he is out to make me look bad, and you along with me." Watson withdrew the newspaper and turned to gather his investigation team.

"Then get me some answers, Moondog, and get them for me five minutes ago. The mayor has already 'invited' me to his office for a 'discussion.' I am getting it from all ends." The captain's voice grew louder while his finger shook in Moondog's direction. "I need answers. I need the killer locked up in my jail by tonight. You hear me, Watson?" Roudebush bellowed while he jabbed the air with a fat finger to punctuate his words. Moondog nodded that he heard, then waved for his people to join him.

"Got ya, Captain. Let me pull the team together and see what we have so far. I had two further contacts with the killer, and I want to add those to our investigation board. Then we can try to solve this," Moondog stated.

"Good, get me answers today. Get me answers five minutes ago. My meeting with the mayor is in three hours. I better have some good news for him or it will be bad news for all of us. Everyone works around the clock until we solve this," the captain said, then raised his head and his voice, adding, "Does everyone hear me? Leaves, vacations, and days off are canceled until I have this killer in cuffs." He walked back into his office, slamming the door with a sound that reverberated throughout the room and down the hall.

Moondog motioned for the investigation teams to join him in the back to start assembling all the information. He turned to the photographer and told Patterson that he wanted the photos on the big screen first. Moments later the large, high definition TV was hooked to Patterson's computer, and his digital shots slowly moved from view to view. Everyone sat staring as each morbid shot flashed on the screen. It was Moses that saw a speck in the sky as they looked at the shots of the surrounding homes.

"Stop there. What's that spot in the sky?" he asked while stepping forward to examine it with his eyes as close as possible.

Patterson laughed. "Moondog told me to get every bird that flew by. I did it as a joke, but let's get a closer look." The photographer tightened in on the anomaly and an image came clear.

"That's a damn drone. The bastard was watching us the whole time from the air. No wonder he knew when to call as we left. I had uniforms out searching every house within viewing distance, and that asshole was watching us from the sky." Moondog Watson was angry at himself for not guessing how he had been observed. "Lopez, I want to know every drone that was purchased and sent to someone in this city in the last two years. Every one of them. Then interview everyone. I don't care if it's a six-year-old kid. I want to know everything about every one of them," Watson barked. He motioned for Patterson to turn off the photos and the television.

"Let me fill you all in on a few more details. I went to my shop, Abby Road, to do some research. I knew that the grapefruit she was holding was a reference to an obscure book written by Yoko Ono called *Grapefruit*." He tossed the evidence bagged copy of the book onto the table. "I was reviewing my copies at the store when this note was found inside this one. I want it dusted for prints, and find out what magazines the words came from. As you can see, it simply told me to answer my phone. Then my phone rang. It was another Beatles song called "The Continuing Story of Bungalow Bill." The words are simple; 'Hey, Bungalow Bill, what did you kill, Bungalow Bill?' I believe our killer has given himself a name. Hell, he did his own press release photos, so why not give himself his own name?" He handed the note off to an officer, who left the room to have it examined for fingerprints.

"That tells me that he is an egomaniac. He doesn't want some evil villainous name given to him by us or the newspapers. He wants to be known as Bungalow Bill. That's where we stand right now. Let's comb through everything. What else did you find at the crime scene?" Watson asked the officer in charge of the crime scene search.

"I did as you asked and searched every brick between the phone booth and the crime scene. I was able find a few faint impressions of a shoe heel. It is nothing like anything I have seen. From the weight displacement they look to be thinner and higher than a normal man's boot, with a pointed toe," he reported. He attached photos of the boot heel impression to the board in front of them all.

Watson looked closely at the picture, then smiled. "They're called Cuban heels. They started out as dance shoes, mostly flamenco, then the Beatles commissioned four pair for their new suit image after returning from Hamburg. They were all the craze in the sixties. I still have mine tucked away in some closet." He paused, and grinned at the memory. "The earliest version of my group, Johnny and the Moondogs, wore them. We all had them, the whole band — and then all the replacement members had to get them, too. We called them Beatles boots, so it really doesn't surprise me that our killer was wearing them." The detective turned back to the officer who had posted the picture. "Find out where they can be bought, and I want a list of everyone who bought recently and locally." Watson stated. For the young men and women on the team, his knowledge seemed boundless. It was no surprise that he would be the lead detective on this investigation.

"How do you think he knew when you would find the note at your store?" a new female detective asked John. Detective Marylee McCarren was young and had muscular definitions to her arms that stretched out from her short-sleeved uniform as she raised her arm to ask the question. Her honey blonde hair was pulled into a high ponytail that poked out of the rear hole in her ball cap. It bobbed as she wrote his answer in her notebook.

"I had a surveillance system installed. We are going over the system to see how Bungalow Bill hacked it. The note could have been placed there anytime over the last week from when I first opened. Although, I don't remember anyone looking through the books. I will review my surveillance videos to see if we can come up with anything," Moondog answered. He also thought to himself that a drone flown outside his store window could have given Bungalow Bill the same seemingly omniscient knowledge.

"Could it have already been in the book when you bought it?" Detective McCarren questioned further. Moondog was starting to like this new detective. She was persistent and thorough.

"I like how you think, but no. I go over every item I buy to verify its authenticity. I would have found it then. What else have we found?" He pointed to Lopez as he stood in the back.

"I got the call records from the phone booth. You were right. The call to you came from there. I am tracing all the other calls made in the last few months. Most were dead ends, but there were two that stood out. One was to a used record shop on Main Street in the old part of Bettendorf. The other was a tobacco and magazine store just down the street. They were made the same day, and only a few minutes apart," reported Lopez.

"Good work. Have you sent anyone down to interview the store owners?" Moondog asked.

"That's my next step," he answered while scribbling in his note book.

"Lopez, you do that as quickly as you can. I think you have a grasp on what we are looking for. Did we find anything under the body at all?" Watson asked, with a glance towards the lead investigator from the crime scene team.

The man responded next. "I used a wet vac to pull everything off the street. We are sifting through a ton of minutia and haven't found anything yet, but we are not done."

"Call me if you have anything that you think looks interesting. Let's move on to a profile of our criminal. We need to get into his head."

The team was interrupted by an officer entering carrying a postcard.

"Moondog, a messenger just dropped off this postcard for you." The female officer handed it over to John.

He read it and his skin went white. It read:

"Send me a postcard, drop me a line
Stating point of view
Indicate precisely what you mean to say
Yours sincerely, wasting away."

"Shit, he struck again. Process this while I do some research. Moses, Lopez, get the car ready."

CHAPTER 6

One Month Earlier

There was knock on the door at the David household. Charles looked up over his glasses at his wife, Vera, and queried, "Who could that be at this time of night?"

Vera rose from her chair next to the fireplace and walked to the door. She peered through the curtain of the side window and saw a man dressed in a dark suit, white shirt, and black tie. He waved to her and smiled a large, friendly smile. Vera cracked the door open but left the chain on. "How can I help you?"

"I am so sorry to bother you. I was driving home from work and got a call that my daughter was having her baby. Right after that my car sputtered and I looked down and saw that I ran out of gas. I don't know where my mind has been. This has been such a difficult pregnancy, and I guess I have been preoccupied with her health. I was wondering if you had some gas in a can that I can borrow. I will buy some, fill my can, and bring the can back tomorrow after I see that little bundle of joy. They're calling her Vera. Isn't that a beautiful name?" the smiling man in the black suit gushed.

"What a coincidence. My name is Vera, and of course we have some gas in the garage," she answered as Charlie David moved to the door next to his wife.

"If my granddaughter grows up to be as beautiful and as kind as you are, then I will always tell her the story of the woman named Vera that saved my bacon." He smiled again as his eyes filled with moisture. His sincerity and love for his children that showed through with each word touched Vera's maternal heart deeply. She turned to Charlie and motioned for him to move along more quickly with a sweeping brush of her hand.

"I will go get the gas can and meet you at the car. Can't have you missing the birth of a girl named Vera. It is a great name for a great woman," Charles added as he shuffled by Vera and the unlit face of the man, peering between the door jam and the chained door. He moved to the door leading into the garage, flipped on the light, found his gas can, and exited out the main door from the garage.

Vera smiled. The two of them had done a good thing. She truly loved Charlie. They had been married forty years, and she still appreciated his kindness. Charlie had been aging quickly, even though he was a year away before his retirement at sixty-five. They'd already bought the small cottage up north where they would spend summers and weekends. It wasn't exactly *On Golden Pond*, but then again Charlie wasn't the cantankerous old Norman either. He was a good man, better than she could have ever asked for. Vera watched as Charlie carried the can of gasoline to the car then returned to her comfortable armchair, sat down, picked up the newspaper, and began reading once again.

***

Charlie carried the gas tank down to the car at the front of his house. "Just got it today. I wanted to cut grass this weekend if it doesn't rain, but hell, you can have it all and I will get more. Just consider it one good deed for a nice, fellow human being. You can pass on the good will to someone else. What's that phrase? Pay it ahead?" Charlie hefted the full can

28

towards the grinning, friendly stranger.

"Thanks. You have no idea what this means to me. I can't wait to see my little Vera. Let me put the gas in, then I will pop the hood and prime the carburetor while you start the car. Okay by you?" the man asked as he patted Mr. David's shoulder.

"No problem," Charlie said.

Charlie slipped behind the wheel in the car. He was getting ready to tell the man a joke he had heard at the office that day when he felt the needle slip into his neck. He remembered nothing else until he awoke in the basement of an abandoned building, chained to the wall, naked and shivering.

Chapter 7

Moondog Watson opened up his computer to YouTube and typed in the title of the tune, "When I'm Sixty-four." He chose a selection with the lyrics on screen. He listened and read. There had to be a lead somewhere inside that song. As he finished the song he looked up at Moses and said, "He is starving someone to death. How long does it take someone to starve to death?"

Detective McCarren answered, "Between twenty-one and forty days."

"Then I want the missing person records of anyone who disappeared in the last forty days. There can't be that many. Give me all the Quad Cities records and every little village around us," he said to anyone listening, while continuing to scan the lyrics to the song.

Moses had already picked up the phone. He methodically called each police station in the surrounding area and asked to have the lists emailed to him. As each email popped up he read them off.

The third list had one name that perked up Watson's ears. "I want all the details on that last one you read."

"A Charles David went missing a month ago. His wife said someone had run out of gas in front of their house. Mr. David went out to put gas in the car and never returned," Moses read off.

"Call the wife and tell Vera we need to talk to her now,"

Watson commanded as he rose from the desk chair.

"How did you know her name was Vera?" Moses inquired.

"It's in the song; 'grandchildren on my knees, Vera, Chuck, and Dave.' We need to talk to her now. She saw the killer, and it is the best lead we have. We have to find Mr. David before he dies. I am guessing today is the last day of the forced fast before it kills him." Moondog circled his upturned finger in the air as he quickly strode towards the door. "Let's roll, Moses, and grab Lopez." Watson was heading towards the door and cars with the vibrancy of a young rookie. He'd gotten his first break in the case.

Fifteen minutes later they were knocking on Vera David's front door. She looked through the window and Moses flashed his badge. Once inside, sitting in the living room, Moondog started to question her in a calm and warm manner, as to not frighten her. "Can you describe the man who kidnapped your husband?"

"Kidnapped? The investigating officer thought he just ran away from me. He accused me of being a bad wife, and dismissed the whole case as a mid-life crisis. He insisted that Charlie must have a mistress that he ran off with. Now you say kidnapped?" she fumed. "Why would anyone kidnap Charlie? We have no money. We had to scrimp and save just to buy the cottage up north."

"Did someone check the cottage for him?" Watson asked, still holding her gaze.

"Yes, my son went up two weeks ago and said there was no sign of anyone being there since we had all gone up for a weekend months ago," she answered, but with her puzzled look was growing more concerned.

"Where is the cottage?" Moondog asked as he took

her hands in his to reassure Vera that her information was important.

"About an hour north on White Isle Road," she answered. "243 White Isle Road, to be exact, but he isn't there." She pulled her hands back as one flung to her open mouth. "Do you think he is still alive?" With that question tears welled up in her eyes.

Moondog shook his head yes, said his thanks, and walked briskly to the car. He barked at Moses, "I want full sirens and lights. We are getting close. Call an ambulance to meet us, and tell them if the man is still alive then he is being starved to death. That should prepare them for what they will find. Do it now and let's go."

Seconds later the car was jumping away from the curb en route to what Watson hoped would be the capture of Bungalow Bill, and the discovery of Charlie David still alive.

The hour drive was made in forty minutes, the ambulance only a few minutes behind them. Moondog's large body didn't wait for the key to open the front door. He pushed his weight against the lock and the door popped open. Laying in the middle of the floor was the frail, emaciated form of Charles David, but Moonie thought that what was placed around him was odd. Junk food was set carefully and purposely in a spiral around the painfully thin body. "Moses, get pictures before they move Mr. David. Bungalow Bill is making a social statement. Bill is one sick bastard."

Sammy pulled out his phone and snapped shots as the medics were entering the door. Once again, the scene was staged precisely, and Watson bet there would be no clues left behind.

The medics went to work quickly. He was still alive, and they had him up, on the gurney, and out the door to the ambulance in minutes. They gunned their engine and poured gravel and dust into the air as they raced to the nearest hospital. With a prayer, David would make it, but now it was Watson's turn to look for anything left behind or to wait for the phone call. He didn't wait long. He pushed the button to answer when the song started.

> "In my mind there's no sorrow
> Don't you know that it's so
> There'll be no sad tomorrow
> Don't you know that it's so."

Moondog recognized the song, "There's A Place," from their first British album, *Please, Please Me*, but he also knew that it wasn't giving him a clue or a lead, but just a demented killer's insight into himself. He felt no sorrow, and there would no sad tomorrow for Bungalow Bill. Bill felt no remorse for his killing or his torture. Moondog was glad that Charles David was found alive and there would be no sad tomorrow for his family. Now, it was just a waiting game until they could analyze the information they had.

"Let's go back to the David house and tell Mrs. David the good news. Also, get a sketch artist down to the hospital to meet her. I want every detail of Bungalow Bill's face, body, build, and height. I want it all."

Moondog had barely gotten the words out of his mouth when his phone rang again. He expected the next clue from Bungalow Bill, but instead it was Captain Roudebush.

"Watson, I meet the mayor in ten minutes. What do you have for me?" his voice boomed.

"I am happy to report that we were able to save victim number two, but the killer eluded us. We do have an eyewitness that saw him. I am getting a sketch artist to work with her to come up with a picture. My team will add that to the facts we know to see if we can't get out ahead of this maniac," Moondog reported.

"That's better than nothing. It might keep the mayor off my ass for a day or so. You gotta solve this one quick, Moondog, before this guy kills anymore citizens. Good work so far, but work harder and faster."

The phone went dead, and the captain was off to his meeting. Lopez, Moses, and Moondog drove with lights on back to the David house to give her the good news.

CHAPTER 8

The news left Mrs. David in tears. She released her stress with streams of joyful tears and a silent prayer to her god. When she finished crying, Lopez handed her a box of tissues he had found in the hallway. When Vera had finally composed herself, she lifted her eyes to Detective Watson and asked, "What can I do to help you?"

"Tell me about the man who kidnapped your husband. What did he look like? Was he tall? Young? Old? Did he say anything that might have seemed odd? Did he have an accent?"

"I didn't get a good look at him. I first peeked through the curtain next to the door, then only opened the door as much as the chain would allow. I didn't get a good look at him in the dark. He seemed about four inches taller than me." She indicated the height with her extended hand above her head. "That would make him around five foot nine or ten. He was our age, and appeared to be in excellent shape. You know, the broad shoulders, thin waist sort of build. He must have been bald because he wore a wig. I was a hairdresser, and I know a rug when I see one," she relayed to the three detectives, smiling at herself for remembering so many details.

"Could he have been covering his own hair?" Moses asked.

"I guess he could have. I didn't get that good of a look. He was gray along the sides and dark on top. Come to think of

35

it, it did bulge in the back, as if he had hair tucked up inside the wig. He was clean shaven, but he had a beautiful smile. He must have been a real heartbreaker when he was a teen. His eyes were dark, with very little in the way of laugh lines around them," she finished, then sat back in the chair. Her tired eyes told them she had recalled all she could for that moment. Watson patted her hands.

"Thank you, Mrs. David. I have a squad car coming to pick you up to take you to the hospital. Your husband is in very bad shape, but he will live. A little later I'm sending a sketch artist to the hospital for you to work with. The more we know about how he looks, the easier it will be to put him away. Keep trying to remember anything at all. No detail is too small." Moondog reached into his shirt pocket. "Here's my card. Call me if you can think of anything else." Watson placed his business card in her hand, held her hand for a moment, and gave it a snug squeeze. She smiled. The three men drove in silence as they headed back to the station. When they walked into the room, the other cops clapped. The news of saving victim number two had already spread. It was one point for the bad guy and one point for the good guys. Watson called them all back to the situation room to see what else they had uncovered.

The crime scene tech spoke first. "I went through every particle on the street. There was nothing unusual, but the coroner said he found some synthetic hairs when he examined the victim's severed head. And he said it looked like the beheading was done with a sword. He sets the time of death about three hours before she was discovered."

"What do you have on the drones?" Watson asked without looking up from his perch at the head of the room.

Detective Marylee McCarren spoke up. "Since Detective

Lopez was with you, I stepped in to cover that one. Was that okay, Jerry?" She smiled his way. He nodded affirmatively, and she continued. "There were ten purchased by locals. Three were kids, four were schools, one was for a security company, one we can't locate, and the other was for industrial use. Although, that one has hit a dead-end as well. It seems the company went under a few months ago. It was called Best Technologies. We are trying to find out who worked there, who owned it, and where they went afterwards. Not much of a trail was left on them. I plan to go out to their site tomorrow morning and poke through the empty rooms to see if anything was left behind," said the junior detective assigned to that task.

"Lopez, go with her. She is a good cop," Watson said.

He was about to tell them everything he had found out in the last few hours when the door pushed open, and in walked a woman in a crisp black suit and white blouse with just enough buttons unbuttoned to make sure no one confused her for a man.

"Can I help you? This is a private meeting," Moondog said directly to her.

"Agent Trew with the FBI, and I think I can help you," she stated, and followed it up with a smile that was as disarming as her legs.

"I didn't know the FBI had jurisdiction over a local murder," Watson shot back.

"I'm not here to see which one of us has the bigger dick, Watson. I'm a profiler, and a damn good one, with the FBI. I was in town consulting on a case when this one caught my eye. I have a few days off and thought I could help you build your profile. Simple as that. I am here to help, and you are obviously still the lead. Can you use me or not?" she said as she pulled up a chair. She had already assumed that he was going to include her.

"Got a first name, Agent Trew?" Moses requested.

"It's Prudence, but people I work with call me Trew. So, just call me Trew and never call me Prude." She smiled, and Watson noticed her sharp dimples as she did. "I will drop unnoticed into the team," she said as her legs crossed. Moses closely watched her skirt rise. She smiled at him, because she knew exactly what she was doing.

"Let me review everything we found out today," Moondog said, then went over the phone calls, the note, the rescue of Charles David, the scattered unopened junk food, the song clips, and Mrs. David's description before asking everyone to pitch in on building a profile. No one spoke. They looked at Agent Trew for her opinion.

"May I?" she asked as she grabbed the white board marker, then began building the profile. "First of all, Watson, you would make one helluva profiler. I can't believe what you were able to dig up in one day. Secondly, this is like a TV wrestling grudge match. The killer has got it in for you. He doesn't want to kill you. He is trying to prove that he is better than you. You better review everyone you pissed off or put away since you got out of diapers. One of those people will be your serial killer." She grinned at Moondog as she stood only a foot away. Not only did this woman have looks, but she also smelled great. He pulled in another whiff of her perfume.

"We know he is five foot nine or so. He is balding on top with graying sides, with either a mullet or a ponytail in back. I am betting on a ponytail. He is too arrogant and too much of a narcissist to have a mullet. The song bite sent to Watson at the David cottage is a confession. He is a sociopath. He feels no remorse about killing or torturing or any other type of cruelty." Trew wrote each observation on the white board. "The hack of the Abby Road store computer and the usage of a drone tells me that Bungalow Bill is well above normal in intelligence, and very technologically astute. He is vain. That's why he chose his own evil villain name. He won't leave anything to chance. He is methodical, and has been planning this killing spree for a long time." She finished her neat printing on the white board and placed the marker in the trough below. She stared at Moondog and gave him a smile that turned up the sides of her lips, punched dimples in her cheeks, and crinkled her nose. Watson didn't miss any one of those attributes.

"I would suggest that you can flush him out using his own arrogance against him. Don't use the Bungalow Bill name in any shape or form. Don't feed his arrogance. An angry killer makes mistakes. Release no information. Don't call it a serial killer on the loose. Let that shit about a terrorist running free take precedence. That will piss him off. And speaking of the severed head, he used a samurai sword. Yoko Ono's ancestors were samurais." She raised an eyebrow before continuing. "Your killer is a stickler for details so obscure that no one could break his code but another Beatles geek or dweeb totally entrenched in Beatles trivia. Give me some time to review your other materials and we can flesh him out more tomorrow afternoon."

Trew walked back to her seat after finishing with her assessment. Everyone watched her return to her seat—Moses stared a little too closely. He loosened his tie as if the room had suddenly become warm. Moondog excused everyone to go home and get some sleep, then walked over to the FBI agent.

"Sorry for being such a dick when you walked in. Everyone

here calls me Moondog, but feel free to use any term you find agreeable. You know your stuff and I appreciate the help. I do have a question for you." She nodded her permission for him to ask the question. "That thing about the samurai sword. That is very obscure Yoko Ono trivia. I remember forgetting that."

"Listen, I grew up in the home of two total Beatles freaks. That is all they played all day long in the house, in the car, and at the pool. It was in my head all the time, and I mean all the time. My dad was always throwing around trivia like that and testing my mother and me. It was part of what kept us together. I loved my parents." A misty glaze came over her eyes. "I lost them a few years back. The police said it was an accidental hit and run. I've always had my suspicions, but no proof. They never found the car that hit them, the driver, or even a remote clue." She sighed and blew out a long breath. "That night I got a phone call. It was an audio clip from a Beatles song. The song was 'Baby, You Can Drive My Car.' I have a feeling your case is related. I need to be a part of it for my own curiosity."

"Do you need a ride home?" Watson asked. He wanted to know more, and he had a strong urge to get to know more about this dazzling woman.

"No, I need a good, stiff...." She paused and grinned her nose crinkling smile. "Drink."

40

Chapter 9

Agent Trew was staying at the Radison downtown—Moondog followed her car there. His mind was on this woman. She was probably twenty years his junior, but he felt a connection to her. Maybe it was the Beatles trivia knowledge. Maybe it was the fact that her parents may have been killed by the same killer. Or maybe it was because she was drop-dead gorgeous. He tried to keep his mind on the professional side of things, but then it would drift to those long legs, her scent, and that smile. He felt he was too old for her, old enough to have been her dad. He didn't need a relationship at this stage of his life. He had retirement a few weeks away, and his dream business had just opened. Now the Beatle murders had showed up on his doorstep, along with this intriguing woman. He had to stay focused. Prudence Trew was going to distract him at the wrong moment if he didn't keep it professional. But oh, those legs.

Agent Trew stopped in the parking lot and swung one leg out of the car, then the other one. Moondog watched intently before exiting his car. She fumbled in her purse for a minute and pulled out her room key.

"Do you mind if we stay outside for a few minutes? I get so tired of stale office air most days."

"Sure. Maybe you can tell me more about your parents' murders. I have the old gut feeling that we are after the same guy," Watson said as he leaned against the car opposite her.

He wanted to see her face in the parking lot lights as they spoke.

Her forehead scrunched as she thought. Trew exhaled a long breath, then spoke. "My mom and dad were computer geeks from the early days. After working for several of the big companies, they struck out on their own. They did well. They came up with a guidance system for drones a few years back that caught the interest of the Pentagon. Towards the end of negotiations, Dad mentioned he was bidding against another tech company. He never mentioned who it was. After his death I tried to use my government connections to find out who had won the bid. It was all hush hush." She shifted her weight from one foot to another and stretched her back. "One night I followed one of the young government lawyers who had worked on the deal to his favorite watering hole. He bought me a few drinks and I flashed him a little cleavage. The name Besttech came up. Soon after that, the boy lawyer's MILF fantasy faded as I excused myself to go outside and have a smoke. I told him to order us a couple more drinks so he wouldn't follow me." Trew ran her fingers through her hair, fluffing it in the wind.

"I researched Besttech, but soon after they got the contract, the ownership was bought out. The former owner disappeared. All history on Besttech had disappeared along with him. He was able to wipe his identity from all files. I've been waiting for him to surface again." Trew straightened her skirt and smoothed her blouse after the stretching.

As they walked through the hotel entrance Moondog questioned her further. "Why did you think he would surface again? What makes you think it is the same man?"

"Want to get a drink?" Trew asked as she pointed to the hotel lounge. As they sat at the bar Trew began her analysis.

"This guy is a sociopath. He is highly intelligent, and after my parents he had a taste for blood. It wouldn't be long before he would do it again." Their drinks came and she smiled at the bartender before stirring the swizzle stick inside her cola colored Jack and Coke. She waited a moment before starting again. "He is motivated by vengeance. You have crossed his path before, and now, he is out to show that you are weak and feckless. If you were a businessman, he would bankrupt you. Since you are a homicide detective, he has to show you that he is smarter and better. He plans to murder until your reputation is worth shit. You will retire as an embarrassment to the force. That's his goal." Trew signaled for the bartender to fill her glass again, then turned to Watson. "He didn't count on me coming along and throwing a spanner in the works." She went back to her drink and downed it one gulp, then breathed out a sigh.

"You mean Spaniard, don't you?" Moondog quipped.

"Thank you, Mr. Lennon, for that twisted phrase," she said with a grin as she popped the cherry from her drink into her mouth. Moondog was hoping the stem would come out tied in a knot. Instead it came out slowly as she popped the cherry off the end. She looked at him and laughed. "I know what you are thinking, and no, I can't do that."

When they finished their drinks, Watson slipped her his card along the smooth, wooden bar top and said that the team would gather again tomorrow morning at eight. Trew pulled her card out of her purse and wrote her private cell number on the back.

"If anything happens, call me. I want in on the crime scene. I might notice something you don't, and you might have something rolling around in that cute little head of yours that I don't know." She gave a coy wink. "Whoever it is, they can't know more than we do put together. Unless, of course, it's Ringo doing all this."

"He is in town, you know," Moondog said as he pulled bills off a roll of cash in his pocket and dropped them on the bar.

"I wasn't aware of that. Is he playing somewhere?" she asked with quizzical, sparkling eyes.

"Some big charity event at the casino this Sunday night. My dream is that he shows up at the Abbey Road opening. Now, that would be cool," Watson added with a large grin.

"I hope not," she fired back. Watson looked stunned. "Sorry to bust your bubble, Moonie, but having Ringo in town could be just what set this sicko off to begin with. Starkey could be the ultimate attack on his part. A high-profile murder could put Bungalow Bill at the top of the maniac, serial killer charts with a bullet. I think I should let the other Feds know so they can add extra protection." Trew stopped and placed her hand on his arm. He could feel her warmth through his jacket. "Maybe you and I can go to the event as a protection detail." She sighed. "I wouldn't put it past our killer to make a showing there." She slid off her stool and stood an inch from him. He could feel the heat coming off her body and smelled her perfume once again. It was different from anything he had ever smelled before. A hint of vanilla and a hint of citrus.

Watson rubbed his jaw. She was right, and being with her for an evening out would certainly not be an unpleasant duty. He looked her in the eyes. "I will have the captain assign me to it, and you can go as my cover. I think it is a black-tie event. Do you have anything to wear?"

"I'll just wear your black tie," she said with a wink.

John liked a good flirtation. This woman was pushing all his buttons at the same time when he had to keep his mind sharp and on the case. He'd better put his feelings in check, he thought. With that in mind, he rose from the bar, gave her one last smile, then walked out, but couldn't resist swiveling his head and taking another look. She'd known he would, and was waiting. She stuck out her tongue, and on it was the stem from the second cherry from her drink, tied in a knot. Moondog snickered, shook his head, and left, thinking that maybe a little diversion wouldn't be so bad after all.

CHAPTER 10

Moondog walked into the station with an egg, bacon, and cheese biscuit and an extra-large cup of black coffee. Most of the team had already assembled in front of their board. It had been a good night—no new murders had been reported. Bungalow Bill had not struck again. That made the sunshine a little brighter.

"What do we have new today on this case?" he asked.

Moses, who stood next to him, said, "That Fed from last night was right. The coroner matched a samurai sword to the blade that severed her head. We also got her identified as Minh Tam. She was thirty-eight years old and was a part time instructor at the community college. She hung out at the café nearby. Lopez and I are hitting the café, the magazine seller, and the record store this morning."

"Anything else new?" Moondog asked as he took a bite of his breakfast sandwich.

"I'm calling the missing persons people right after our meeting. I don't want us to discount anyone that is not where they were supposed to be. That bothered me about how we handled that old man who was nearly starved to death. I will make sure anyone missing is reported to you right away," said Marylee McCarren, the young ponytailed detective. Moonie liked her. She was sharp and she was proactive.

"Good, Detective. That is the type of thinking that is going to get us one step ahead on this case," Watson said as the door to their room opened and in walked Agent Trew. Everyone's eyes angled towards her.

"Sorry I am late. I wanted to inform my main office as to where I would be for the next how many days. Any new killings?" she asked as she dropped her body into a chair at the back of the room.

"Nothing, but we haven't heard from the missing persons department yet. McCarren, go ahead and get any information that you can now, then update me. Everybody keep your eyes open. Follow up on your assignments and then follow up again. I want nothing missed. Let's catch this bastard before he strikes again. And let's—"

A uniformed police officer banged open the door and pushed fast into the room.

"Detective, a guard from the courthouse just called. A judge was found murdered in his chambers!"

"Shit," was all Moondog could get out of his mouth before his phone rang. He knew it would be Bungalow Bill.

CHAPTER 11

The previous night, Judge Hatalsky had stayed late to look at some papers couriered over to his office late in the afternoon. His superiors wanted an opinion first thing in the morning. Hatalsky thought it unusual, but his opinion would carry some weight behind it. He was the oldest judge still sitting, so his opinion on legal matters was often sought, but never at night. He was supposed to play bridge at the club that evening.

Judge Hatalsky rose from the desk in his office. He needed to grab a cup of the bitter coffee that spewed out of the machine in the employee's lounge. It wasn't good but it had caffeine in it, and that was exactly what he needed to finish the last few pages of his opinion. He walked out of his chambers and down the hall. The marble floors and walls echoed each of his steps back towards him. It was a walk he had made many times before in the silent evenings. Hatalsky pushed open the door to the lounge and flicked on the light. He dropped his coins into the slot and chose a large coffee with one creamer. He had quit taking sugar a few years ago when his doctor informed him that, like most overweight men, he was a diabetic. The judge was very careful, since he planned to do a boat load of fishing once he retired in a few months. He snatched his coffee from the machine and made his return walk to his courtroom and his chambers.

Hatalsky opened his door and had taken two steps into

the room when a thunderous blow came down on his head. He never heard the voice hiding behind the door as it softly sang the chorus of "Maxwell's Silver Hammer."

***

The searing pain in the judge's head thumped as his blurry eyes tried to focus on the figures coming through his chamber door. He struggled to escape, but the bonds were too strong and his age and blood loss had left him too weak. He managed to gurgle a few words through the blood in his mouth. "Who are you, and why are you doing this?"

"Hmm, that is such a good question, Judgy Wudgy. I believe, though, that you are not in any position to be quizzical, or even pataphysical. But, but, but, I have brought two people you might know, and they can't wait to see my new masterpiece." The man pulled the two women, with their hands tied behind their backs and their mouths taped, directly in front of the judge. "Do you remember Rose and Valerie? They're going to SCREAM from the gallery. Not that I, Maxwell Edison, must go free. No, I believe they will scream that *they* need to go free. I don't think they'll even care if you go free." The man calling himself Maxwell pushed the two bound and gagged women into a courtroom row a few feet from the judge. They thumped into the seats with muffled, terrified screams.

"Years ago, you took no leniency, and tonight, I return your ungracious action." Maxwell picked up his silver hammer and tapped the judge's wound, sending shock-waves of pain through the old man's body. Maxwell looked at Rose and Valerie and asked with a friendly, charming smile, "Should he go free?" No answer came through their muffling gags. "I agree. He does not deserve it. He must be punished." Maxwell raised his voice to a bellow on his last sentence.

Maxwell skipped behind the judge and carefully picked up his silver hammer. He raised it above Hatalsky's head in a measured blow that would not kill the man, but would place him in excruciating pain. The silver hammer came down. Maxwell moved around to the front of the judge and, leaning over, placed his hands on top of the old man's. The killer moved his face in close to the judge's and sniffed the air. "Oh, Judge, you are not looking well, and you are not smelling well, either." The judge's soiled suit pants and the yellowed puddle beneath the chair gave away his sheer fear.

Maxwell then glanced back over his shoulder at Rose and Valerie, and an innocent, childish smile came across his face. His eyes twinkled with delight. He stood up straight and walked with long strides and exaggerated arm swings towards them. As he arrived, he pushed Rose to one side and dropped his body hard in between the two. They tried to move away, but he grabbed a knee from each of them and held them still.

He smiled at Rose and then at Valerie. "Neither of you remember me, do you? That's good. If you remembered me then I would have to kill you with my hammer." He pulled it from his coat pocket, raised it to Valerie's forehead, and tapped her lightly. Fear shot to her eyes and she recoiled. He giggled, then turned and did the same to Rose, who had a similar reaction. "Don't fear the hammer, ladies," he reassured them. "It is for the judge, and that teacher, and of course...." He paused. "Joan. Can you believe that Joan broke up with me even before our first date? Moondoggie will find her eventually, along with that wicked teacher." He sighed and ran his fingers down both of their knees before arising and skipping like an insane large child back toward the judge.

"It is getting late, and once again it has been 'A Hard

Day's Night' for me. I must wrap up my little work of art and get some rest." Max gave an exaggerated yawn and stretched his arms outward into the air. He walked closer to the judge, a sneer forming on his face as he moved around behind him, walking his fingers along the old man's shoulder. Once more he raised his hammer, singing, "Bang, bang, Maxwell's silver hammer came down upon his head." He dropped the hammer twice on the judge, cracking his skull. "Bang, bang, Maxwell's silver hammer made sure that he was dead." With the song finished, Maxwell took a full swing at the top of the judge's head, spraying blood and brain matter in every direction. Satisfied with his final blow, Maxwell moved along side of the dead man and ran his finger through the oozing brain matter around the judge's eye. He raised his finger to his mouth, where his tongue snaked out, and licked it clean. He looked at Rose and Valerie to get their attention. "Umm, yellow matter custard dripping from a dead judge's eye."

A boyish figure moved down the dark, far aisle, leaving the judge's chamber door wide open. Maxwell smiled at it when he saw the bundles of files being carried away. He gave a cute little wave and turned his attention back to the job at hand.

He walked briskly towards the back. As he passed Rose and Valerie, he smiled. "I told you that I wouldn't kill you with the hammer. I keep my promises, ladies." Then he reached into his waistband and pulled out a pistol. "Maxwell kills with a hammer." His high pitched, childish tone changed to a deeper male voice. "But Bungalow Bill uses the classic Colt 45. Thanks for joining me. It was fun," Bungalow Bill said as he cocked his head and smiled. He pulled the trigger twice, sending a bullet through the heads of each of them. Bungalow Bill pushed the doors open and danced the old Bandstand

Stroll down the hall.

CHAPTER 12

The courthouse was a block from the police station. Watson didn't wait for his car, his partners, or the other team members. He barreled down the sidewalk at full speed, and was directed into Hatalsky's courtroom by a local guard. He wasn't prepared for what he saw, but he wasn't surprised either. It was gruesome. He took a few steps towards the judge before Moses, Lopez, and Trew burst through the doors behind him. As he reached the dead man's blood coated body, he glanced down at the silver hammer that had been dropped in his lifeless lap. He stopped and stared, starting to make mental notes.

Agent Trew stepped up behind him. "This has to be 'Maxwell's Silver Hammer,'" she said.

"The Moondogs cover this song in one of our sets. I know the lyrics well, but help me piece together the clues. He is obviously the judge, and I am assuming the two women are Rose and Valerie." John turned to Moses and spat out, "How were the two women killed?"

"My obvious guess is a gunshot to the head at close range," Moses returned.

"As soon as the coroner identifies them, I want a complete background check. They have to have a connection to the judge, me, or Bungalow Bill. I want to know everything about them, and I mean everything. There is a twisted connection to our killer, and it may just lead us to him," Watson commanded as he moved in closer to look at the top of the judge's head. When he looked back to the opening doors, he saw the crime investigation team wheeling in the equipment. "Ladies and gentlemen, I want every inch of this room, and the judge's chambers, gone over with double effort. Something is here. I don't know what it is, but my gut says something was left behind."

Trew moved up close to him and quietly offered, "What bothers me is what is not in the room."

Moondog stared at her, wondering what she meant.

Trew continued, "We have the judge and we have Rose and Valerie screaming from the gallery, but I don't see the teacher and I don't see Joan, who was quite quizzical. There are two more bodies out there killed with the silver hammer. We need to find them and work the clues together, but how?"

Watson called Lopez and McCarren over to him. "Agent Trew has a good grasp on the background to the song 'Maxwell's Silver Hammer.' In that song there are two other killings. I want you to start with all the schools in the city and see if any teacher didn't report to work today." He rubbed his temples with the fingers from both hands. "The other person to search for will be a woman named Joan. She is somehow tied to the words quizzical and pataphysical. Search the newspapers for any linkage between those words. Try the Internet as well. We need any leads back in our hands in an hour. Get going, and keep me posted."

Moses caught the two as they left to hand them copies of the two female victims' fingerprints. He knew from experience that Moonie wanted their identification immediately. He strolled up to Detective Watson and waited for further instructions.

Moondog was still rubbing his temples from the oncoming

tension headache. He looked at Moses and said, "Sammy, this is a really shitty mess, and I don't mean the courtroom. While we were out slapping ourselves on the back for saving victim two, Bungalow Bill was busy killing three, and most likely five, people. I need you to go over every scumbag that Hatalsky sent away." He pointed at the officers standing around watching in the back of the courtroom. "Get a couple of uniforms on this right away. There is a link between Hatalsky and the killer. Also, retrace the judge's steps last night. There has to be a reason that he was staying late, and maybe there is a clue in that reason." Watson clasped Moses behind the neck and pulled him towards him, and whispered, "And I need you to look back at our cases to see whose cornflakes I pissed in. Somewhere in my own past there is a clue."

Moses nodded, turned, and exited the room. John "Moondog" Watson walked towards the prosecutor's desk and sat down. He stared at the judge without speaking or blinking for ten minutes. Patterson the photographer stood next to him for a few minutes, waiting for him to acknowledge his presence. Agent Trew saw that she no longer could help Moondog and left for the station.

Finally Moondog looked up at George and said, "That old guy has been on the bench since I was a teenager. I bet me and every one of my friends stood before him in our day. He was a mean old cuss. He even sent a few of my buddies to juvie for a few months." Watson paused, then stared at George and said, "Yeah, same protocol as on Blue Jay Way. Something has been left behind for me to find. I want thorough photos even after the bodies are removed. My gut tells me something is here."

With that said, Watson pushed his big, athletic frame up from the desk and headed for the judge's chambers. Maybe the clue is in there, he thought. A few minutes later he left the judge's chambers, but with a slight grin on his face. He now knew something that Bungalow Bill could not perceive that he knew. He had a clue, and it was a damn good one.

CHAPTER 13

John Watson walked slowly back to the police station, his hands in his pockets and half smile on his face. Before stepping into the station he drew in a deep breath, blew it out, and pulled the door open. He nodded to the officers guarding the metal detector, and they nodded back. He strode towards the elevator and waited. When the doors pinged open he stepped inside and pressed the button for his office floor. As the door slid shut a hand reached in and blocked the closing door. He knew the hand and the red nails that tipped it. It was Prudence Trew.

"Did you find anything?" she queried with her mouth turned up in a smile. Her tired looking eyes warmly danced up and down his body. He liked the way she looked at him. He liked the way she looked.

"Once again we came up with nothing. Bungalow Bill continues to stay one step ahead of us. I am hoping that the team has discovered the names of the other victims."

"Are they searching for a missing teacher?"

Trew moved closer to him. She felt his heat and he felt hers. Watson shrugged to indicate that he didn't know as of that time. They finished the rise in the elevator in silence. Before the door opened she touched his arm. It was electrifying. The woman was seductive and smart. He liked that as well, but he also questioned her obvious interest in him. He was obviously old enough to be her father.

The doors slid open and they walked into a room filled with the noise of men and women on the phones compiling information. Moses was the first to approach them. He extended his handwritten notes towards Watson. "Moonie, the girls were friends from grade school. Rose Perez's maiden name was Kingston, and Valerie Howell's maiden name was Everly. Both of them were your age, and went to high school in Bettendorf."

"I know where they went. They were two years behind me. I knew them casually," Moondog said as he scanned Moses's notes. Inside his guts turned. Two more people were dead, and he couldn't help but hang the blame on his own head. The killer was making another statement, leaving another clue, but John wasn't putting it all together. It didn't make sense.

Trew stepped forward and quietly asked about the teacher character from the song, "Maxwell's Silver Hammer." Moses looked her way. John noticed he was straining to keep his eyes on her eyes. He didn't want her to know what he wanted to look at were the freckled breasts thrusting between her white blouse with the two top open buttons. Watson grinned. He knew it was an effort for Moses. Trew was truly a beautiful and attractive woman. He reached out and grabbed Moses's shoulder and turned his attention towards him. Sammy reluctantly moved his eyes towards his boss.

"Anything on the teacher?" Moondog asked.

"Not yet. We are calling every school to see if one did not show up for school and did not call off. It is laborious, but something will turn up soon. Did you find anything at the courthouse?" Sam questioned without looking back at Prudence.

"Have to wait for forensics, but I found nothing," Watson

lied as he slipped Sam's notes back into his hands. He patted his shoulder to say "good job," then headed for his desk. Trew fell in behind him. He sat and she pulled up a chair across from him.

"The girls were from your past. How well did you know them?"

"Not that well. They hung out with a couple of the band members from the early incarnation of Johnny and the Moondogs. Myself, I had little contact with them except to say hello," he said, then went silent before smacking his hand on the desk. A startled Trew looked up at him. Worry crossed her brow and set in her eyes.

"You can't blame yourself. You're not the killer. You're simply the target. He is trying to get at you and keep you off balance," she reasoned as her hands fell on top of his.

"I have to figure out who is angry enough at me and crazy enough to pull all this off."

"And rich enough," she added.

"This is the damn Quad Cities. There aren't enough monumentally rich people around here. Maybe we should question every one of them, but I do not remember crossing anyone with that kind of money," he said as he sucked in a breath and pushed it out of his lungs. Watson scratched his head hard to stimulate the brain cells before pushing himself away from his desk and standing. He yelled to anyone listening, "Anything on the teacher yet?" No one answered. "What about a Joan, anything?" No one answered.

It would be a long morning.

CHAPTER 14

"I have never let my schooling interfere with my education," said Mark Twain. Jean Gilson kept that quote above her kitchen sink and lived by that intention. She had retired from teaching third grade at the Mark Twain Elementary School nearly a decade before. Jean spent a year outside the classroom, but she missed it. She missed the kids. She missed the challenges. She missed watching her students grow into model citizens, and prayed for those who became far less than what she knew they could be. Jean had signed up to substitute teach in the same system that she'd left. Gilson was able to pick and choose the days she wanted to work, and the days when she just needed to educate herself with a trip to the museum. The night before she'd agreed to substitute at her old school in her old classroom. Miss Gilson couldn't wait.

She had laid out her clothes and packed her lunch when a knock came on the door. Jean walked to the door, but as all seniors had learned, she was cautious. It was evening, and she had few visitors and no family in the area. She called out, "Who is it?"

"Flowers for Jean Gilson," came the voice from the other side of the door.

Jean flipped on her porch light, moved the curtain back, and peered out the window. In front of her house sat the van from Knees Florist shop. She looked over and studied the smiling man at her door holding the potted plant in his hands. He saw her staring at him and his smile grew.

"Sorry for the lateness of the delivery. Our delivery guy called off sick. I am just filling in, but I wanted to make this delivery. I'm Billy Houk, and I had you in third grade many years ago." His smile grew bigger.

"Oh my, Billy?" she responded. "I never would have recognized you all grown up." She popped the locks open and yanked on her sticking front door. It swung open and Jean smiled at Billy. "How have you been?"

"Had some health problems lately, Miss Gilson, but am doing fine now. It is great to see you. I wanted to say thanks for being such a great teacher. The wife, Debby, and I still do the square dancing that you taught us," grinned out Billy as he handed over the flowers.

Jean Gilson was remembered by her students because the whole school day with her wasn't just about learning in books. She made the day fun by pushing the desks against the wall once a week and teaching them how to square dance. No student walked out of her room without knowing they were loved, and without knowing how to dosey doe.

Miss Gilson took the flowers from his hands and turned around to place them on the hallway table next to the upstairs steps. When she turned her back on the boy, he crept up from behind, humming a little tune as he pulled the silver hammer from his coat. Billy raised his arm, and as it descended he broke out singing, "Bang, bang, Maxwell's Silver Hammer came down upon her head. Bang, bang Maxwell's Silver Hammer made sure that she was dead."

Blood splatter sprayed the walls, the flowers, and the table before her, and streaked across the delivery man's face. Jean pitched forward and fell onto the table, then onto the floor. The potted flowers skidded across the hardwood and settled in the corner. She never read the note, and never saw that it said Rest in Peace. The delivery man turned and lithely skipped through the door, pulling it shut behind him. In another moment he was in the truck and heading towards the alley, where he would dump the stolen vehicle after leaving the body of quizzical, pataphysical Joan.

CHAPTER 15

Two hours passed in the police station without any word on a missing teacher. Moses began recalling each school. As he prepared to dial, a call came in to his extension. "Detective Moses," he said. Then he listened. "Why wasn't it reported when I called before? ... Okay, so Miss Gilson is an elderly substitute. I get that part, but was she supposed to be there? ... Do you have an address for her? ... This is not a privacy issue, ma'am. She may have been attacked and need help. ... Yes, please put me on with your principal," Moses said, then waited. He listened as his hand scribbled the address of Miss Jean Gilson on his scratch pad. He said thank you and hung up the phone. "Moondog, I've got the address of a missing teacher," the detective said as he waved the paper in the air.

John Watson crossed the room quickly and snatched the white paper out of Moses's hand. He read it, then stumbled back and sat on a nearby chair. Watson mumbled, "She was my third-grade teacher — my favorite teacher. She is the only teacher I kept in touch with." Watson's emotions rose to his face and his eyes swelled with tears. "Moses, Lopez, Trew, let's go, and McCarren, call the crime scene team and dispatch whoever is available to this address." He handed the officer the paper and steamed his way through the crowd of officers towards the door. Trew, Lopez, and Moses were on his heels.

Watson had his siren blaring and his lights on, in hopes that he would find old Miss Gilson well — or at least, still alive.

Once the group reached the home, the four disembarked quickly, jogging up the front walk. Moondog knocked, but the force of his knuckles pushed the door open. He saw her lying on the floor, where a pool of blood had formed and coagulated around the wound in the back of her head. He knelt beside her and felt for a pulse. It was faint—barely there—but it was there. The other three had already fanned out to check the home room by room. Moondog pulled his cell from his pocket and dialed 911. He instructed the dispatcher on where to send the ambulance, and made sure the dispatcher knew that if the EMT's were not there in ten minutes, he would have all their jobs. The 911 dispatcher understood and put an ASAP priority on the call.

Moondog sat beside his former teacher and held her hand. "The ambulance is coming, Miss Gilson. You have got to hang in there. I will be here holding your hand until they arrive. It's Johnny Watson, Miss Gilson. I am here." Then he went quiet and sobbed.

"The place is clear," Lopez reported as he approached the woman on the floor and the tough, hardened cop holding her hand and weeping. Watson looked up and nodded his thanks, and went back to his vigil. He heard the sirens of the ambulance roar up to the house. He glanced at his watch. It had been eight minutes since his call. As they rushed in, Moses helped Moonie to his feet.

"She is barely alive, Moses, but she is still alive. Once she is out of surgery I want a guard on her room 24/7. If Bungalow Bill knows he bungled this killing, I believe he will try again. In fact, tell everyone to just report it as a death." He grabbed Moses by the shoulder and pulled him around so he could look in his eyes. He wanted an assurance that his orders would be followed. "I want it kept quiet that she lived.

Make sure the two EMT's understand that, and make sure the hospital understands that." Moses nodded and left in the ambulance.

Moondog Watson was sitting on the steps next to the hallway staring at the pool of drying blood. He dropped his head into his hands and shook it. This one rattled him. Bungalow Bill had made it a personal battle. Moondog gritted his teeth. He never lost a battle, he thought, and he wasn't about to start now.

He stood as the crime scene team arrived on the porch. The photographer, George Patterson, was the first one in. "Any instructions, Moondog?"

"Yeah, I want everything. Scour the place for clues. And Lopez, I want to know where the flowers came from, when they were picked up, and how the guy paid for them. Get a description of the guy and then get me a sketch of that face. I want this bastard in my hands by tonight," he barked. Then he walked out of the house, down the walk, and sat in the car. Lopez and Trew followed without saying a word.

It was a quiet and morose ride back to the station. Moondog spoke to no one as he entered and went directly to the room that held his board and the existing clues. Reports and photos had been added to the collection of the other killings and attempted homicides—the pictures and reports from Hatalsky's courtroom. Watson dropped into a chair and lifted the pages. He went through the motions of studying the details, but his head was foggy. He stared down at the blood that was still on his hands from when he had picked up Jean Gilson's hand. He wept again.

Captain Roudebush pushed the door open, then shut it behind him. He pulled up the chair next to Moondog and sat. He said nothing—he didn't need to say anything. Moondog had sat in silence next to him when Roudebush's daughter was found with her throat slit two years before. They both knew that words could not express their grief. Somehow, though, having that friend sitting nearby allowed them to share the pain that twisted like a serrated knife in their hearts.

Chapter 16

Roudebush stood and exited the room. Moses was the first to enter and sit next to Watson. Speaking quietly, he said, "Jean Gilson is still in surgery. She was admitted under a false name. Once she is out of surgery and in her room, the officer on the scene will call here with an update. The doctor said it would be touch and go for the next few days." Moses stopped and waited for a comment. Moondog was silent, so he continued. "We found the delivery truck. It had been stolen yesterday afternoon, and of course, it was wiped down and sanitary except for a slight trace of blood under the installed shelves. We did get a boot imprint from our killer stepping in the blood at Miss Gilson's house. It matched the one at the Blue Jay Way killing. It was a Beatle Boot, as you called it." Watson gave no comment, so Moses continued. "Should I call the team in?"

John "Moondog" Watson stirred, lifted his head, and croaked from his hoarse throat. "Yeah, you lead them. I don't think we will find any clues or missteps in Bungalow Bill's work. The solution to all this is somewhere in my past. I need to sort that out myself." He slapped Moses on the knee and stood. "I'll be back later, but call me when Jean is in her room. I want to see her." He walked towards the door, then stopped and pivoted towards Moses. "Anything on our quizzical Joan victim yet?"

Moses shook his head from side to side.

Watson walked slowly out of the room through the collection of good cops smiling at him. Without acknowledging anyone he left the room, grabbed an unmarked car, and headed for his brother Matthew's house.

When their mother died, Matt had inherited the family home. All the brothers laughed. Matt was the baby, and of course their mother would give him everything. Matt Watson ran his computer forensic business out of his home, and was usually at the old homestead. Moondog pushed the doorbell, then laughed at himself. The old bell hadn't worked for the last thirty years, and he still found himself pushing it out of habit.

"Hey, big brother, what can I do for you?" Matt queried as he swung the ancient front door open, allowing his brother to walk by him.

"You once said that Mom had boxes of our childhood memories. Do you still have mine?"

"I have all of them in the attic. Do you need it right now?"

"Yeah, I do. It is important or I wouldn't bother you while you're working," John responded as he stared around at the four walls of the living room where he'd grown up. Matt could see something was bothering his brother. He didn't ask. He walked up the stairs to the hatch to the attic. Watson dropped his body to the couch and stared at the corner where the old black and white television had sat when he was a kid. It was on that screen that he watched the Beatles on *Ed Sullivan*. It was on that screen that his desire to play their songs had germinated. It had been a special moment in his life, but as he reflected on it he felt remorse. People were dying because of him, and somehow his life journey, steeped in Beatles lore, was being used against him and innocent people.

"Hi, Johnny. Would you like some coffee? Although by the looks of you, I think bourbon may help a little more," Matt's wife Melanie said as she walked into the room. She was drying her hands on a dish towel. Mel was very perceptive.

John smirked. She was right—he needed a good strong drink, but the coffee would serve his purpose better. "Thanks, Mel, black coffee would be nice." He smiled at her before she turned to walk back to the kitchen.

"Are you excited about retirement?" she yelled from the kitchen. "And the big opening of Abbey Road this weekend?"

"Retirement has been postponed, but the opening has not," he called back, then rose to the edge of the couch. He had not thought about the opening. It had come out of his mouth without reflection. Then he nodded to himself and said to Mel as she brought the coffee in to him, "Yes, ma'am, Abbey Road will open on schedule, and I have a feeling there will be some special guests there. You two are still coming, aren't you?"

"With bells on our toes and rings in our noses," she joked, then lowered herself into the easy chair across from him. She studied him as he sipped his coffee. She knew something was wrong and didn't want to pry, but this was her brother-in-law. She had put up with the crazy antics of all five of the Watson boys. She leaned forward. "Is the retirement postponement because of the terrorist that the newspaper is talking about?"

"More or less," he answered, then said no more. She got the hint that that topic was closed. She felt John's wall go up, and she was relieved to hear Matt thumping down the stairs. He turned the corner with an old box in his two hands.

John looked at him and nodded thanks. "I take it my old baseball cards have miraculously disappeared?"

"Well, not quite disappeared, but they are certainly in the safe. I didn't want them to walk off like Eddie's did. I am protecting them from you and the others," he smiled. It was an old joke from their childhood. John lifted the box from Matt's hands and headed to the dining room table.

"Is it all right if I work here? I need to be away from prying eyes for a few hours."

"Have at it, big time detective. I've got some research to do in my office, and I think Mel was going grocery shopping. The dining room is all yours," the brother said as he headed to his office and closed the door. John heard Mel's car start and leave the driveway. He was alone with his thoughts, and not one of them was pleasant.

CHAPTER 17

John's mother, Adeline—commonly known as Addie, maiden name Flannery—Watson had been the last child born into a large brood of Irish descendants. Her brother was a cop. Her dad was a cop. Her grandfather was a cop, and her great-grandfather was a cop. Johnny Moondog grew up in a family of cops. From the time he was able to remember he'd heard stories, often enhanced by Irish whiskey, of the exploits of the Flannery men in uniform. He'd had two choices for a career—he could be a rock 'n' roll star, or he could be a cop. He'd chosen correctly. As a cop he was very good. As part of a Beatles cover band he was good, but as a rock star he was mediocre.

John pulled the collection of papers from the beat-up old box that Addie had put them in. There were cards he had made her, the first coloring page from his first day at grade school. His first lock of hair wrapped tight in parchment paper. They were memories, good memories, and Watson smiled. Life had been simpler growing up. You either played ball in the street or you watched the old black and white TV.

About halfway through the box he found what he was looking for—the stack of classroom photographs. The fresh smiling faces were fading with age and yellowing, but they were still there. He found the one from third grade with Miss Gilson. Watson picked up his pen and note pad, and began writing. As he stared at each face, the cop forced himself to remember every kid and everything about them. He skipped over the girls. Mrs. David's description had been plain that the killer was a male. And as far as John remembered, the girls in his class were all still women. No transitioning for his generation.

He wrote every boy's name down and then started the elimination process. Jimmy McAdams lived two streets away from him. He was short and had gained a little weight over the many years. Physically he didn't fit. Watson scratched his name off the list.

Marvin Montgomery sat next to Jimmy in the photo. Marvin was the only black kid in the class. Once again, Mrs. David's description said white male; and besides, Marvin had moved to Atlanta after college. Watson scratched his name off the list.

David Gettings was next in line. David was the first drummer in his band that formed four years later in seventh grade. Back then they were the Daydreamers. They were terrible, but they did appear on the local cooking show, *The Kitchen Corner*. It was their career highlight. Soon after that Mrs. Gettings made David quit the band. His grades were slipping, and he needed a scholarship to go to college. It was a smart move on her part. David was now the city controller in Chicago.

Dwarfish Eric Greer was the last boy in the first row. Eric was smart and cool, but he never got above five foot tall. He was now a successful psychiatrist in New York. He might be worth talking to after this was all over. Watson felt he would need a little psychoanalysis by that time.

Fred Riley, the school's top jock, started the second row. He was a little league hero, and went on to play triple A baseball. He never made it to the big show. The last Watson heard, he was coaching high school baseball somewhere in Nebraska.

Lowell Fulton, known as Mrs. Fulton's Folly, was a great friend and a funny guy to be around. Even until the end, when cancer took him, he was upbeat and fun to hang around with. John scratched his name off the list, along with the next two, who had died in an auto wreck and in warfare. Next was his best friend, Billy Houk. Billy had married Moondog's cousin Debbie. There wasn't an evil bone in his body. He scratched his name off.

The last three were rather unknowns to Moondog. Walter "Corky" Hodgdon, who was born with a cleft palate, had moved soon after the fourth grade. Jimmy McCall was a weird kid with an abusive and controlling father. Watson didn't know where Jimmy had ended up.

The last picture was Jelly Jerry Jefferson. Jerry had gotten his nickname because all he would eat were jelly sandwiches. No peanut butter, no butter, just white bread and grape jelly. Jerry had replaced Dave Gettings as the drummer for the Daydreamers, and was still the drummer when they transitioned into Johnny and the Moondogs. He was never a good drummer, and didn't get any better from the day he joined, but he owned his own drums, a sparkling red kit from the Sears catalog. It looked good but Jerry played poorly. Jerry was a handsome young man, and the girls swooned over him after they played. He was definitely the most popular in the group, but quite honestly, his terrible playing had held them back.

The Moondogs had pushed John to cut him and replace him with a high energy young guy called Gary Shansky. John finally did, and Jerry never spoke to him again. It was a tense time for the band, but the years had shown that Jerry's drumming did hold them back. Watson lost track of Jelly Jerry after high school. He knew he'd gone off to school somewhere out east, but after that they never crossed paths again. Jerry never came to high school reunions, and his parents had moved to some gated community a decade ago.

John rewrote his list with the three names. Jimmy McCall was at the top. Walter "Corky" Hodgdon was second, and Jelly Jerry was third. He put that photo away and went through the other items his mother had kept. There were scrap clippings from newspapers from when he had played football, and the ads placed in the newspapers for the Daydreamers, and later the Moondogs. It had been a rare trip down through his ancient memories. When he was finished, John packed up the box and called to his brother Matt.

CHAPTER 18

"Hey, Matt. I'm done out here. I'm going to swing by the cemetery to visit Mom and Dad's graves."

Matt stuck his head out the door and asked, "Do you mind if I come along? It has been several months since I did that, and I'm kind of missing old Addie these last few days."

John motioned to his brother to come along. The two moved towards Watson's Crown Vic and roared off towards the cemetery just a few miles away. Matt didn't say a word the whole trip, but as they arrived at the cemetery gate, John's phone rang. He touched the button to put the phone on speaker, then said hello. No one was there. John was about to hang up when he heard a song come through the speaker. It was a Beatles song called "Your Mother Should Know."

The song trailed off. Matt stared at his brother. Watson stared back and said nothing. Bungalow Bill had struck again. This time it was even closer to home.

"What's that all about, Johnny?" Matt quizzed as he poked his finger towards the phone.

John debated as he finished the drive toward the gravesites. Should he tell Matt all that was going on, or should he pass it off as nothing? Matt was too smart to pass it off as nothing. As the two climbed out of the Crown Vic, John moved close to Matthew and began the long explanations of his recent case. He summed it up by saying, "He is watching my every move, and I think it is by drones."

"I take it that you think it could be someone from your past," Matt said as he pulled a clump of grass from around his feet and threw it, blade by blade, towards the flowers that decorated their mother's grave.

"That's why I went through the box. I wanted to see the old pictures of my third-grade class. There were only three guys I could not eliminate."

"Is it time for Matman and Bobin to get back together again?" Matt referenced the old days when Johnny had babysat his younger brother and they played their version of Batman and Robin, called Matman and Bobin. John was Bobin, and he had pushed Matman around the room in his red toy metal car. That bond still held them together.

"Before that song I would have said no, but it is time for Bobin to call in Matman on this one," John said, while slipping the small page of three names he had written on a piece of paper into his brother's hand. "Find me everything on these three. I want to know everything since they graduated high school. I want a trace of all their financial dealings, credit card use, and locations for the last couple of decades. I want everything."

"Matman is on it." After they paid their respects the two walked back to the car and John dropped Matt off at his house, then headed towards the police station.

John "Moondog" Watson walked into the station and motioned for Moses to join him in an open interrogation room. He filled him in on the photo, the three names, and the song on his phone. Moses stared into space, then ran his fingers through his dark, thinning hair. "Do you think Matt will come up with something?"

"I hope. It has to be one of those three, but I haven't had contact with any of them for decades. I don't even know where they are."

"At least one of them is in the Quad Cities right now," Moses said as he stood.

"That is what I am thinking. If one of them is then maybe we should contact everyone else from my third-grade class to see if they have had contact with one of the three. I'll have Matt scan the class photo and send it over."

Moondog stood and rolled his neck, trying to relieve the tension building up in his shoulders and head. As he opened the door to leave, Moses grabbed his shoulder and turned him around. "I think you should cancel the grand opening of Abbey Road this Saturday."

"I thought about it, but I am sure Bungalow Bill will be there. I am adding extra cameras so I can catch everyone walking in and out. We will have a face after Saturday night," Watson said with a glint of hope in his eyes.

"What about the Ringo Starr concert on Sunday night? The captain wants you to head up the security detail, and he wants to have Agent Trew there as well. Are you up for it?" Moses questioned.

"I'll be there with bells in my nose and rings on my toes," Moondog responded, then walked out of the room with Moses behind him.

Prudence Trew walked through the door a moment later, wearing tight Levi's and a tight white T-shirt covered by a black leather motorcycle jacket. She had pulled her hair back in a ponytail, giving her face a fresh, young look.

Moses drew in a breath and whispered out, "Ouch, she is scorching hot."

She sauntered over to Watson and looked up at his face. "You look tired and tense. How can I help you? Do you want to go have a drink, or something else?" she asked.

Her eyes danced with a flirtatious smile while she licked her lips. John got her point, and yes, he could really use both to break the tension in his muscles. He knew what he wanted from her, but he couldn't think through why such a beautiful young woman was interested in a tired, old cop. He decided not to come to a conclusion and just ride the wave as it came.

"Yes, that sounds good." He had turned to grab his keys off the desk when Moses ran up to him.

"Moondog, Miss Gilson is coming out of her coma. We need to double time it to the hospital," he whispered.

Watson leaned into Trew and said that he would have to take a rain-check on the drink and other things. Before he spun away, she grabbed his arm and looked him disappointedly in the eye. "Can I come along? I want this guy as bad as you do."

He smiled back and nodded up and down. The three walked quickly to the Crown Vic and raced to the hospital. The elevator seemed to move slower than usual as it climbed to the third floor. Once the doors opened, the three nearly ran down the hall to room 307. The guard posted at the door recognized Moses and Watson and opened the door for them. Trew followed, flashing her FBI badge.

A doctor stood over the battered old woman. He glanced up from her chart to see the three holding badges out for him to see. The nurse next to him smiled and said, "Dr. Tobias, this is Detective John Watson." They shook hands.

"I understand that she is coming out of her coma. How long before I can talk to her?" Watson asked as he moved his body to stare down at his former teacher.

"I need to run a few tests and make sure she is strong enough to talk. Can you give me two hours to do that? Then I will need to be there when you speak. She is really at a very tenuous stage, and I want to do nothing to send her back into a coma." The doctor's serious stare gazed into Watson's eyes, then moved to Moses, and finally lingered on Trew. She smiled at him, and he smiled very warmly in return.

"We can do that." Watson didn't want his disappointment to show. "We will leave and you can take care of her. She is an old friend and my favorite teacher from when I was a kid, so do everything you can to help her." Watson knew that adding a personal connection to a patient was always good for getting an extra special measure of care from a doctor.

He turned to leave, allowing Moses and Trew to go ahead of him and out the door. Once the door swung shut he turned to the doctor, pulling him to other side of the room, and whispered a change in plans. When finished he walked out of the room, joining the other two at the elevator doors. He smiled and said that he had wanted another moment with Miss Gilson to whisper an encouragement to her. Trew touched his arm and reached for his hand as they rode down the elevator. Her perfume was rising to his nose. He liked it; it was a scent he would never forget on a woman he would never forget. But not for the reason she had hoped.

Chapter 19

Watson called the Moondog band members to reschedule the practice to a later time that night before walking into the small restaurant. While Watson, Moses, and Trew sat in a coffee shop drinking coffee and waiting to return to the hospital in another half hour, a thin, tall, and homely elderly nurse came on duty on the third floor of the hospital. Her scrubs hung loosely on her frame. Her make-up was done but poorly applied, as if she had been late for a very important meeting. Black cat-eye glasses rode low on her nose. With all the movement between visitors and medical professionals, she may have gone unnoticed except for the clicking of her thick heels on the linoleum floors. The sound drew the attention of the young officer guarding the door. He looked up and saw the nasty looking woman with a harsh scowl drawing her expression downward. She approached him and stood with one hand on her hip and a small plastic cup of pills in the other.

"I am here with the patient's medication. Don't you need to frisk me or something?" the nurse said as she flung her body against the door, raising her hands and spreading her legs. She tipped her head back and gave him a demure smile while batting her eyelashes.

He grimaced. The old nurse was repulsive.

"No need. Go on in." He went back to reading his newspaper and she pulled the door open. A few seconds later the door flung open and banged the hallway side of the wall. The nurse screamed at the cop. "Where is the old lady?" She pounded her fist against the door. "Where did they take her?" Spittle flung from her angry, screaming mouth.

The cop dropped his newspaper and gave an I-don't-know gesture, then rose to apprehend the woman as were his instructions. She took a step back, looked at him with a smile, and asked a question. "What's black and white and red all over?" Before he could answer the nurse pulled a scalpel from her scrub pocket and slashed him across the neck. His blood pumped out quickly, spraying red blood across the black and white print of the newspaper he had held. He dropped to his knees, clutching his neck. The homely nurse made a dash for the stairwell, but stopped at the door. She turned and called back to him. "A newspaper with your blood on it!" Then she was gone before the head nurse and a security guard could get to the dying police officer, clutching his wound in a futile attempt to stop his rapid blood loss.

The security officer saw the head nurse lean down to help. He then pulled his weapon and jerked open the door to the stairway. The officer heard the clatter of thick heels hopping down the metal stairs and echoing off the walls. He moved cautiously to the steps and peered down. The security officer heard singing, and then heard the first-floor door fly open. He reached for his radio and alerted officers on the first floor about the nurse in blue scrubs on their floor.

The security officer took each step down cautiously, watching and listening. The tension drew heavy lines into his brow and along his mouth. His hands grew moist with sweat. When he reached the second floor landing he saw the blue scrubs and a blonde wig discarded at his feet. His earlier description would help no one in locating the killer.

He finished his climb downward and found nothing in the hall, until another guard came quickly around the corner. The other officer shrugged with his palms up to demonstrate that he had seen nothing. They had done what they were trained to do. It was time to put it in the proper authorities' hands and move on. The security officer sighed in relief. His training had never touched on what to do when facing a crazy killer.

Ten minutes later Moses raced in the front door of the hospital, followed by Watson and Trew. They had heard the call for the police and responded. He knew he would be too late to catch Bungalow Bill, but he wouldn't be too late to get a description of the perpetrator. He was hoping the young officer, who was cut, would live, but he also knew that the Beatles killer struck for death, not for injury. Moses headed up the steps to see about the officer down while Watson and Trew held up their badges.

"Did anyone see what happened?"

The security guard that followed the killer down the stairs approached him. "I did, sir. At least a part of it." He wobbled on his feet and backed against the wall to steady himself.

"Can we go to your security office? I want everything you saw, and heard, and I want to see security video of the scene," Watson told the man as he placed his hand on the guards back to steady him as they walked. He could feel him trembling. The recent encounter with Bungalow Bill was obviously more than he was trained for, and more than he'd expected as a security guard in a hospital. Trew followed them towards the security office.

As the guard pulled open the door, another guard sat at the console staring blankly at them. Watson looked back at him and said, "I'm Detective John Watson and this is FBI agent Prudence Trew. Are you able to rewind the videos of the attack?"

The man stammered out a yes, then turned back to his console and began setting up the screen shots for Watson and Trew. John sat the first guard down and took the chair directly opposite of him. "Trew, will you find this guy a glass of water?" he said calmly at he looked up at her. She moved out of the doorway and down the hall. "Now tell me what you saw."

The guard pulled in a deep breath and blew it out. He spoke low and quietly in an attempt to keep himself calm and clear. "I didn't notice the nurse at first, but I heard the clunk of heels on the floor. The place reverberates with that type of sound. Most nurses and doctors are in soft soled shoes. Less noise and better traction is what they tell me." He paused and took another breath, then started again. "I looked up and saw a tall, thin nurse in blue scrubs heading for the officer. She appeared to be carrying a cup of pills for the room he was guarding."

"What color was the hair? Was it long or short?" Watson asked as Trew pushed the door open with the glass of water in hand. The guard took it and gulped half of it fast before talking again.

"Blonde and straggly, but that doesn't matter because I found the wig in the stairway on the way down."

Watson stopped him. "Is it still there?"

"I suppose so. I didn't pick it up. We were taught not to tamper with evidence. I left it as I found it, along with the blue scrubs covered in blood." The guard took another sip of water, then continued. "The next thing I heard was the room's door bang open and the nurse yell something about where is the old woman from inside. The police officer stood to restrain her. I saw a flash of something shiny, then the officer crumpled to the floor. I watched his blood pump out of his neck as I ran to him. A nurse was with me, so I headed to the stairwell."

He stopped again, and Watson could tell he was thinking. He said nothing, but placed a smile across his lips to show that the guard was doing well.

"I drew my weapon. I am certified and it is legal for me to carry it."

That cleared up the pause in the guard's statement for Watson. He didn't want to get himself in trouble with a gun charge.

"You did the right thing. What happened next?" John could see the tension leave the guard's face.

"I moved down the steps slowly. I got about two steps down when I heard the door on the first landing bang open, then slam shut. I stopped to alert the guards on the first floor to be looking for a tall, thin blonde nurse in blue scrubs. That is where I screwed up. Ten steps later I found the wig and the scrubs on the second-floor landing. I had everybody looking for a nurse, and the killer just walked out without a second glance." He dropped his head in his hands and sighed.

"You did the right thing. No one could have known he would take them off. Was there anything peculiar? Did you hear anything odd?" Watson questioned.

The guard snapped his head back up and smiled. He had remembered something that might be helpful. "Yeah, the sick bastard was singing a song as he left the stairwell."

"What song was it? Did you recognize it?"

"Kind of. It was something my mom and dad used to play when I was growing up. It was an old song. I'm pretty sure it was by that group Paul McCartney was in before Wings," he remarked.

Watson looked at Trew and she stifled a laugh.

"Do you remember any of the words that he sang?"

"Something about a hole where the rain came in. That is about all I remember," he answered, then slumped back in his chair. Trew mouthed the words "Fixing a Hole" to Watson. He nodded his head in agreement.

Watson turned to the other guard and asked to see the video. It wasn't clear, but the man exiting the steps gave him his first picture of Bungalow Bill. He asked for all of the videos pertaining to the attack to be placed on CD copies. He wanted one, and he wanted Trew to get the FBI to look at the other.

When they exited the security office, Moses was leaning against the wall across from them. "Officer Krauser didn't make it. The cut was to his jugular vein. It was clean, deep, and on purpose. I have the CSI team in the hallway and in the stairway. We should get something from the scrubs and wig. There is always a little telltale DNA left behind with a wig."

"Who has the wig?" Watson asked. An officer near them walked over.

"Detective, I searched for the wig and blue scrubs. They weren't in the stairway. Should I search again?" he asked.

Watson grimaced. "No, because while we were chasing down leads, Bungalow Bill walked back into the one place that no one would expect, then walked out again with our evidence." Watson smacked the wall in frustration.

The three headed back to the police station and split up. Moondog planned to head towards Abbey Road. The grand opening was Saturday, and Johnny and the Moondogs were playing. It was Wednesday, and that was a practice night for the band. At least that was what he told them. Instead, he headed back to the hospital to talk with Jean Gilson. He'd had the doctor move her to a different room under a new assumed name. There was no uniformed guard, but Jerry Lopez sat in the hallway like any other family member watching every move towards her door.

When Watson left the elevator on the fourth floor, Lopez dropped in behind him. "Anything happen up here?" John asked.

"No. All the action was on the third floor from what I gathered. Doctor Tobias said to contact him as soon as you got here and he would go in with you." Lopez dialed the doctor's number and told him they were ready to go in. Three minutes later Tobias appeared around the corner.

"You certainly called that one, Detective. She would have been an easy target in Room 307." The doctor put his hand on the door to push it open. He turned to the two cops and whispered, "She is still very weak. Be patient and be quick."

Watson took four large steps to the side of the bed. Jean Gilson slowly rolled her head his way. Upon recognizing him she smiled weakly. He gripped her hand and applied gentle pressure to say how glad he was to see her. Her eyes brightened. He moved his head close and kissed her cheek. She smiled again.

"I have to be a cop now. I want to know what you saw," he whispered. His digital recorder was on and he laid it on the bed next to her head.

Gilson was slow in her speech. She was very fortunate that the hammer had hit the skull on a part of the brain that did not affect her speech or her memory. But she was still weak, and the words came out slow and hoarse. "He was delivering flowers to me. He said he was Billy Houk. I believe Billy was in your class. It wasn't Billy though. I sort of recognized the face, but it wasn't Billy's." She paused and the doctor held the glass of water. She drew in a drink through the straw, then began again. "I would recognize the face if I saw it again. There was something about his eyes that I remember, but I don't recall much more." She stopped again and smiled at John. "I do remember you holding my hand until the ambulance came. It made me want to hold on to my life. You were always a good boy, Johnny."

Watson's eyes filled with tears. He fumbled in his pocket for his phone, and had his brother Matt email the school photo to him. He pulled it up and began talking to Jean. "I think the guy who tried to kill you was from our third-grade class. I pared it down to three possibilities. Walter 'Corky' Hodgdon, Jimmy McCoy, and Jelly Jerry Jefferson."

Gilson closed her eyes, thinking. "Not Walter. There was no hair lip. Jimmy was always a train wreck waiting to happen. Jerry? Let me think for a moment." She closed her eyes.

At that point the doctor stopped the interview. "The drugs cause her to fall asleep without warning. It will be several hours before she awakens. I will have your partner call you at the first indication that she is coming around. I know it is important to get your answers, but it is more important to keep her alive," Tobias said.

Watson shook his head in agreement. She had at least narrowed it down to two names for him.

The three exited the room and Lopez resumed his watchful vigil in the lounge down the hall. Watson headed to Abbey Road for the evening of practice.

CHAPTER 20

He unlocked the front door for the other three to go in and set up. Most of the equipment had been there since their last practice, and it was also the last time they'd talked. As John unpacked his guitar he looked at the others and casually said, "I want to change the set that we planned for the opening. It might take us a little longer tonight than usual to dust off some of the ones we used to play." John intended to send Bungalow Bill a message in song, much like he was doing to John. He knew he would be there in some capacity. He had to send a message back in a way that the sick killer would understand. It was time to start getting a few steps ahead of his nemesis.

His drummer, Gary, looked at Moondog, questions running across his face. He had known John the longest, and their friendship had spanned a lot of years. He knew his friend, and he wondered what was going on in Moondog's head. "John, if you want to change the song set then I am with you. I am just wondering why."

"I want to send a message to someone that I know will be listening. I can't say more than that," John said to the three Moondogs before flipping on the toggle switch to his amp. He said no more, and the others didn't ask.

The Moondogs had been together for a long time. John Watson had led them from the beginning. His bassist, Jimmy Z, had been with them since the day he used a jig saw to cut his old guitar into a four-string bass. Moonie liked his commitment, and he had been a long-time friend. Jimmy Z was also the local school superintendent. His students had a hard time filtering it through their minds that the top teacher in the district was also a long-time rocker.

Guitarists came and went in the later years before the original Moondog lead guitarist had rejoined nearly a decade ago. Jake the Snake was possibly the best guitarist in the Quad Cities, if not in the two-state area. His playing was perfection, and his style was unequaled.

But it was the drummer, Gary Shansky, that had become the glue for their sound. The first drummer, Dave Gettings, was good, but had to leave the group to focus on school many years before. His replacement, "Jelly" Jerry Jefferson, had never fit in. Watson had been looking for another drummer for two years before seeing Gary playing in a group called the Domars. The next day "Jelly" Jefferson was history.

"We need a playlist, Moonie," Gary said as he moved up to him. Moondog looked at the others, pulled a piece of notebook paper from his pocket, and spoke.

"Here's what I want to do. Saturday is getting pretty personal to me. These songs are going to send a message to someone, and I don't want to go into that any more than I have to. First up, we do our typical opening set with 'I Want to Hold Your Hand,' 'Please, Please Me,' and, of course, 'She Loves You.'"

The Moondogs relaxed. They were all songs they had done hundreds of times. Moondog paused. He shook the paper in his hand and straightened it with the other hand. "I want to move Sgt. Pepper up a few songs, followed by a tribute to Ringo. As we all know, Sunday night is Ringo's concert at the i-Wireless Center Hall in Moline." Moondog paused and smiled. "Who knows, he may even show up at our opening

Saturday night. Fat chance, but who knows." He grinned at them. "Then we'll do 'With a Little Help from My Friends.'"

"So, what are the changes?" Jimmy Z. asked.

"I want to do 'Bungalow Bill,' and close out with 'I'll Get You'," he answered.

"Haven't done those in a while, Moonie," Jake said. "We better run through both a few times tonight."

"My thoughts exactly," Moondog said as he picked up his guitar.

CHAPTER 21

Friday morning's sunlight broke through the window of the Bungalow Bill task force room. Watson carried in his coffee, blowing on it to cool the scalding liquid. He placed it and the morning newspaper on the table, and walked to other side, pulled up a lone chair, and sat. He took a sip of the coffee. His practice had run late the night before, and his body felt the lack of sleep and the weariness of his task. It was time for him to attack back. It was time to take the offensive. The problem was that his clues were too scattered and unconnected to put him on the right track. He needed a break in the case, and he needed it soon. He unfolded the paper and was scanning the front page for any crimes he may have missed when his phone rang.

"Watson," he said sharply.

"Detective, this is Dr. Tobias—"

Watson interrupted, "Is she all right?" His voice reflected his fear and concern.

"Yes, John, she is fine, but my hospital administrator and the board are not fine. They have given me an edict— well, actually an order. I am to move her out of this hospital immediately. The police officer death on our campus has caused a severe drop in our bed population," Dr. Tobias calmly stated.

"What about their frigging Hippocratic oath and all that shit?" John reacted as he tossed the newspaper across the room.

"Detective, I have already worked out the details. I can do it safely without harming Ms. Gilson, and without anyone knowing who she is or why she is being transferred. You have to trust me on this one," the doctor's voice pleaded.

Watson blew out a breath and raked his fingers though his hair. "I guess we have no choice. Make sure she is safe, and don't even tell me where you've taken her." He paused and rubbed his temple to ease the oncoming tension headache. "When are you going to do this?"

Tobias breathed a little easier and answered, "Within the next thirty minutes. I want to do it fast. My best nurse and I will be in the ambulance. She will be safe."

"Let me know when it is done. And Doctor…." He paused and drew in a breath before continuing. "Jean Gilson means a lot to me. This move to a new hospital has to stay just between us. Do you understand?"

"Yes," came the doctor's answer.

Watson pressed the end button on his cell phone as he looked up at the door. A shadow crossed the partially open door to the task force room. He called to the person outside the door. "Come in." No one had knocked, but he wanted them to know he knew they were there.

The door pushed the rest of the way open. Agent Prudence Trew stepped inside as she slipped her phone into her pocket. "Hey, John, I just wanted to check-in before I went to the bureau office to talk to the chief about getting reassigned to this case."

"You didn't have to wait at the door. You could have just walked in," he said.

"I just got here when you said to come in. I thought you had gotten all clairvoyant on me," Trew said. Her voice was throaty and husky. He liked it. She approached the other side of the table and dropped her palms face down at shoulder width onto the table. She leaned in, and with concern asked, "You look bad. Are you all right?"

Watson struggled to move his eyes up from her deep cleavage. His first attempt was retarded by the freckled globes protruding from her obvious lace bra and so close to his face. He finally won the battle and looked at her face, which wasn't bad either. "Late night practice with the band. I need lots of coffee today." His body started to warm and a bead of sweat formed on his brow.

Her hair slid from behind her ears and dropped into Watson's face. She put her hand underneath it and pushed it over the back of her head. Her perfume filled the air. John breathed it in and sighed. Without thinking or filtering his reaction, he said, "I love the perfume. What is it?"

Trew grinned with a smile that twisted up at the end. Her eyes twinkled and her nose wrinkled. "I got it in a small boutique back in Pittsburgh called Erica's Exotic Scents. It is their private brand called *Have Mercy*," she answered with a giggle in her voice as she stretched her neck in close to his face.

"Beautiful," he commented. "And the perfume isn't bad either. Appropriately named. Is it Mercy with a C or an S?"

"Good one, Moondog!" Her mouth opened and she licked her lips before straightening her body to a full standing position. "So, is there anything new?"

"No," Watson answered as he stood up, facing her. "All is quiet on the Bungalow Bill front." He moved around the desk, saying, "I'll walk you out to the door."

Watson placed his hand on her back. Her body was warm, almost hot. The heat penetrated though her suit. She turned her head towards him and winked. Watson knew where it was going from there and smiled back. He wasn't unhappy about it.

Prudence Trew moved away from him and walked slowly, with swinging hips, towards the door. After a few steps she turned and said, "Goodbye, Johnny." He thought, yep, this was going somewhere.

Once she exited the door, Watson turned to Moses. "Sammy, I need you to—" He was stopped mid-sentence by the captain swinging his door open.

"Watson, quick, get in here. I got a bunch of local political big-wigs on my phone, and they want a report from you right now," he bellowed.

"Just a minute, Captain," John said as he held up a finger.

"Now, Watson, that's an order." The captain turned and stormed back into his office.

"Wait for me, Sam. I've got something important for you to do," Watson said as he went into the captain's office. Twenty minutes later, after he had summed up the recent developments for the men and women on the conference call, he hurried back into the big room filled with officers at their desks. He glanced at Sammy and called for him to follow him. Once they were in the elevator he spoke. He wanted no other person to hear what he was to say.

"The doctor called. He is moving Miss Gilson to another hospital right now. Get down there and follow him. Keep enough distance that no one would suspect that you are following them or that you are even interested in the ambulance. Just follow. Keep your gun at ready, No one knows, but I'm not taking any chances at losing an old friend, and the only eyewitness we have."

The doors opened on the first floor and Moses hustled to

his car, roaring out of the parking lot. Watson headed back up the elevator to check on a hunch he had.

***

Outside of the hospital, the doctor and his handpicked nurse were climbing into the ambulance. He'd wanted to go outside of his network of associated facilities, but the time factor constrained him to stay within his own system. The best facility, and the most unlikely, was across the Mississippi in Rock Island. Unfortunately, the bridge over the river was under construction. It would take an extra thirty minutes to make the drive. He couldn't chance using the lights and siren — he didn't want to draw any more attention than necessary. The doctor tapped the shoulder of the driver and directed him to Trinity in Rock Island.

Five minutes later Moses pulled into the emergency room parking lot looking for the ambulance. He saw nothing, but decided to wait just in case the doctor had not left yet. After ten minutes he called Watson.

"John, when was the doctor to make the transfer? I am here and there is no ambulance and no doctor. Should I go inside and check?" Sam queried.

"The doctor must have left already. I don't know where he was headed. Make a few phone calls to ambulance services and find out if they have anything en route to a hospital in the area." Watson paused as he bit his lip. He hoped that Moses was just late and that the transfer was happening without a hitch. He spoke again, "Yeah, call those ambulance services. I am sure that everything is fine. No one knows about this besides you, me, and the doctor, but check out the emergency vehicles anyway." He pushed the red button on his phone.

Five minutes later Moses called back. "Nothing en route, Moondog, but if I was a gambling man I would bet on the

95

other Trinity in Rock Island. With the traffic on the bridge, I might be able to catch them if I use my lights."

"No. Let's wait for the doctor's call that the transfer has been made." Watson took a deep breath into the phone. "This kinda shit puts my stomach in knots. Keep me posted."

Watson rubbed his temples after putting down the phone. He pushed himself away from his desk and was walking towards the bathroom when his phone rang again. He hurried back to it and snatched it up after five rings.

"What is it now, Moses?" he answered. He was perturbed, but at the same time he was hoping it was good news.

It wasn't Detective Moses. Instead it was a song—one he knew well. The tune and words of "Baby, You Can Drive My Car" blasted from the phone's speaker, followed by three pops undeniably from a small caliber pistol. After so many years on the force, Watson knew what he'd heard. He dropped into his seat like a man that was hit by a blind, roundhouse right. His phone fell on the desk still playing the song, and his head fell into his hands. Bungalow Bill had struck again—but how did he know? How did the bastard know something that no one else knew?

CHAPTER 22

The ambulance eased onto Interstate seventy-four headed for the river. Their driver was whistling—the doctor had no idea what song or why. Maybe it was the stress of constantly dealing with emergencies and horrendous accidents. EMS drivers often existed under high pressure. Maybe the guy was just relieved that he didn't have to hurry. He didn't have to turn on his lights. He didn't have to weave in and out of traffic or deal with people that refused to pull over. Maybe the guy was just relaxed. It didn't matter why he whistled. It was disconcerting, but Dr. Tobias was more concerned about his patient getting safely to Trinity in Rock Island.

The doctor wasn't watching when he felt the vehicle take an off ramp and slow down. "What's the problem?" he asked.

***

"Those idiots back at the hospital didn't shut the door properly. I can't have the three of you rolling out into traffic. That would reflect terribly on my driving record. It will only take a minute." The driver swung his door open and strolled around the ambulance. As he reached the back door, he pressed a button on his MP3 player and dialed Old Moonie's cell phone. He casually removed the small .22 caliber revolver from his pocket. He opened the door and a smile stretched across his face.

Dr. Tobias looked up at the grinning man, and suddenly the shock hit him even quicker than the first bullet. The second

97

went into the forehead of the nurse. The third ended the only eyewitness's life.

He didn't bother to push the doors shut. He wanted it found the way he had left it. Placing the gun back in his pocket, he stripped off the rubber gloves and walked over to a parked car. It was running, and the driver waited for him to get in.

"Is it done?" the car's driver asked calmly, as if asking about buying a gallon of milk.

"Yes, I fixed a hole where rain got in." Then the killer giggled at his own joke. "Back to the Batcave," he said, while pointing to the road with a gesture of his thumb.

The car eased out and hit the on ramp of the rest area. In another few minutes they were merged into the thick of the traffic, struggling to get over the one lane bridge.

***

Once Watson recovered from his shock, he straightened himself in his chair, picked up his phone, and called the Iowa Highway Patrol. They had already picked up a call about an abandoned ambulance at the rest area on I-74. He dialed Moses. "Sammy, Bungalow Bill hit again. He got Jean Gilson, the doctor, and a nurse. The ambulance is in the rest area off of I-74. Assemble the team and I will meet you there." He paused. "Sammy, did you tell anyone about this?"

"Hell no, Moonie. Maybe the doc said something before he left. Maybe Bungalow Bill was watching the hospital all the time. Lotsa maybes on this one, but I'm not one of them," Moses answered. "I will call Lopez and start the investigation team rolling and meet you there."

All John could do was sit. He wanted to cry. He wanted to scream. He wanted to kill that bastard, Bungalow Bill. He would get his chance, but it probably wasn't going to be this day. Pushing himself away from his desk again, he grabbed his sports coat and walked quickly towards the door. Where was the leak? He wondered. Where?

As he walked out he saw Detective McCarren's desk. He stopped and looked at the box on top of her desk. He turned around and saw an officer nearby. "Where's McCarren?"

The officer stopped his filing and turned around, held his hands up in the air, and gestured. "Don't know, Moonie. Captain told me to clean out her desk. She quit. Didn't even come in to do it. Just left a message on his voicemail. Ain't that a pisser?"

"Too bad," Moondog said as he shrugged on his coat. "She was a good cop. She had a future here for sure." Then he walked out, got in his car, and drove to the rest area. He took his time. It was an avoidance measure that he often used when he was facing something personally unpleasant.

As he pulled in, Moses walked up to him with his pad out. He was ready to go over his notes, but Moondog shook his head no. There was no need. Any clues would not be in the ambulance. He stared at the parking area. "Sammy, could he have walked out of here?"

"I don't see how. The fencing between here and the neighboring homes prevents an easy exit. I have two officers looking for anything unusual in the grassy areas," he answered.

"If he didn't walk out then he had to have a car here, but there was no time to set that up. He must have an accomplice that picked him up. At least that is what I'm thinking, and it also answers some other logistics questions for me." Moondog paused. He drew in a breath and then asked Moses, "Who found the vehicle?"

"The woman over there next to the squad car. She said she

pulled in, saw the door open, and walked up to the ambulance. Saw the dead bodies and threw up," Moses reported.

"I need to talk to her," Watson told his partner as he moved towards the woman. He could see she was still visibly distraught. He needed to be as calm and comforting as possible to allow her to relive the scene as she'd driven in. Moses matched him stride for stride.

"Mrs. Drake, this is our lead detective, John Watson. Detective, this is Mary Drake." After the introductions, Moses moved back a few steps and Watson moved closer, placing his hand on her shoulder.

"It must have been a horrible experience for you. Are you starting to feel any better?" he asked.

Mary Drake struggled to give him a smile. "Thank you for your concern. It was like someone punched me in the stomach when I saw it. I am so sorry about throwing up on your crime scene."

"I did it too when I started out. No big deal. Are you feeling well enough to answer a few questions?" Watson spoke slowly and calmly.

"I guess so. I really didn't see much," she said, trying to smile bravely.

"Did you see anyone walking away from the emergency vehicle?"

"No. My car and the ambulance were the only ones here."

"Did you see a car pull out of a parking spot?"

"No," she answered, then paused. A memory was coming to her. Watson waited. "There was a car on the on-ramp. It was too far away to see anything."

"Was it a big car, compact car, dark car, light car, fancy car?" he probed.

"It was dark, and it wasn't one of those little Japanese

things. I don't know much about cars. It was about the size of one of the cop cars. That's about all I remember."

"One last question. What about tail lights? Was there a broken tail light? Think hard and tell me anything you saw."

Her eyes rolled up as she desperately tried to access her memory. Mary started to shake her head from side to side when a flash came into her eyes. "Yeah, there was something. When the car accelerated smoke came out of the tail pipe. Then it was gone."

Watson touched her shoulder again. "Are you okay to drive? I can have one of my officers take you home." John was concerned.

"I will sit here until I feel up to driving, or I'll call my husband, Bill, to come get me. Thank you for your concern." She smiled as he handed her his card.

"If you can think of anything call me, and only me," he told her, squeezed her shoulder, and walked away. By the time he got back to Moses, Agent Trew was standing next to Sammy.

Moses asked, "Did she see anything?"

"No, not a thing. She came too late. There were no cars in the lot and nothing on the ramp," he answered.

"Maybe she will speak to a woman. You guys can be pretty intimidating sometimes," Trew offered.

"Don't bother. Nothing there." Watson dismissed her offer quickly. "In fact, you would be a better help to me if we go have a bite to eat and talk this over. I could use a sounding board, and I don't want to be alone. Jean's loss has hurt me badly," he suggested.

"You mean, have dinner together? I thought you'd never ask," Prudence answered. "Where at, big guy?" Her question was flirtatious and filled with promise for the evening.

"Don't care, but it has to have a bar and big steaks. Have you been to Sneaky Pete's in LeClaire?"

"Don't even know where LeClaire is or what it is." She paused and touched his arm. "I'll drive so you can drink, but I will need directions. Is that okay?"

"Nah, believe me, I won't be drunk. One drink is my version of heavy drinking. I think I need to talk more than anything, and a big, juicy steak sounds good. I'll drive, and I'll have Moses take your car back to the station. We'll pick it up there afterwards. How does that sound?" Moondog reached out his hands for her keys. She smiled and pulled the small ring from her coat pocket and dropped it in his hand. Moondog walked over to Moses and gave him instructions. He patted him on the back and strolled back to where she waited.

"Do you think it will be fine if I leave the car there overnight?" Her eyes looked at his. Promise and pleasure was behind them. His lips rose into a grin. Then he noticed that another button had popped open on her white blouse. He really liked this girl, and he hoped that he could see the rest of her that night.

Moondog opened the door for her and she slipped in. Her tight skirt rode up on her nylon clad legs. Even her thighs were sexy, he thought. He slid into the driver's seat and started the engine. For the next twenty minutes he grinned and talked. He talked about third grade and Miss Gilson's class. He talked about her square-dancing lessons, how he hated them, and how bad he was. Then he grew quiet. Glancing over at her he said, "I was so bad that when it came to doing a school assembly, I wasn't part of the square dance group. They made me do the hokey pokey. I had to shake my booty before the whole school." She laughed and touched his arm. "It was the

102

greatest embarrassment of life, at that time."

"Are you scarred psychologically because of that one event?" she asked.

"I'd say yes. I have kept myself from shaking my booty since that day. Fortunately, all the kids, parents, and teachers were watching little Eric, who seemed to relish in the fact that his fat, little ass shook better than anyone's. They looked at him and laughed." Moondog's grin grew into a big smile. "I don't think anyone even noticed me. I was in the back row and Eric was out front. I try to gain solace from that thought."

Prudence Trew laughed at the end of the story. She waited a few beats after ending her giggling, then reached to the top of his leg and squeezed it. "Maybe you can show me that booty dance later. I promise not to laugh, and from what I've seen, you have a very nice booty." A lecherous smile grew across her face. Moondog reacted, but it was not in any place she could see at the moment.

Once in LeClaire, Watson pulled up in front of the restaurant. He started to slide out of the seat, but remembered he had on a favorite J. Garcia tie. He pulled it off. Trew looked at him for a second, then said, "I like that tie. Why are you taking it off? Are you getting ready for later?" She smiled a half smile that crinkled her nose.

"Just the opposite. I really like this tie. It was one of Garcia's earliest designs. Sneaky Pete's doesn't like ties. If you are wearing one they cut it off and staple it to the ceiling." He folded the tie carefully and placed it on the console. "It's a casual restaurant and bar. It gets a little rough sometimes. It's a throwback to the older 'river rat' bars that used to line the river. LeClaire has gone upscale, but the steaks at Sneaky Pete's are the best around."

"Good. Maybe I'll get to kick some redneck's ass. This

whole thing with Jean Gilson has got me as mean as cat piss," she remarked as she opened the door and swung her long legs onto the sidewalk. By the time she was standing, Watson was at her side. "LeClaire looks like a pretty cool, artsy-fartsy town. How do you know it so well?"

As he pulled the door open to Sneaky Pete's, he answered, "My daughter and her kids live up the street. I used to come often to see my grandkids."

"Did something happen that stopped you from visiting?" she inquired while walking across the dim-lit room.

"Not really. They are in Europe for her husband's job." Watson found them a table in a darker corner of the dark room and pulled a chair out for her. "I planned to go see them after I retired and after I opened Abbey Road. Abbey Road will open on time, but our friend Bungalow Bill has definitely slowed my retirement plans." Moondog sat in the chair next to her. A moment later a waitress sauntered up.

"Hey, Moonie. How ya doing tonight?" she asked as her long, wavy blonde hair slid down across her shoulder.

"Been a long day, Jackie. Give me a double bourbon on the rocks," he said, then glanced away from the waitress towards Prudence.

"Sex on the Beach, please," Trew responded with her sexiest smile.

"Not much of a beach here near the river, but if that's what you want, I am sure Big Johnny here could take care of your needs," Jackie tossed back with a dry wit and smile that crinkled her nose.

"Do you know that from experience?" retorted Trew.

"I've tried, honey, but the big guy is not easy to catch," Jackie told her as she smacked John on the shoulder with her note pad. "I sure wouldn't have said no if he'd asked."

The waitress paused, then repeated the order. "One double bourbon on the rocks and a wishful hope of rapturous bliss coming up."

"I like her," Trew stated as she grabbed the menu the waitress had left on the table. "From what you said, I take it that steak is what I should order. I'm in the mood for a big piece of meat."

Moondog laughed and glanced down at his menu. When Jackie returned with the drinks they both ordered steaks. At that point, Trew asked the question he was waiting for. "How are you feeling after the Gilson killing?"

"Not good. I feel like this guy is always a step ahead of me. He seems to know things before I do. I wish I could catch a break, but one just isn't coming my way." He stopped and sipped his drink, then continued. "To be honest, I don't want to talk about it, Bungalow Bill, or this case. I want to just enjoy the steak with some good company."

"Okay by me, Moondoggie. Let's talk about something else. Tell me some stories about Johnny and the Moondogs, and all the groupies that follow him around," she quietly whispered.

John told her stories until the steaks came, then told her more stories as they ate. The two laughed most of the evening before finishing up their dinners. John paid the bill, left Jackie a large tip, and walked Trew to the sidewalk. He stopped and asked if she wanted to take a walk along the river. She nodded and put her arm in his. For the next half hour, they walked without saying a word.

Moondog stayed silent as they drove back to the Quad Cities. He was heading for the police station so Trew could pick up her car when she put her hand on his arm. He glanced over and she looked at him with a longing stare.

"Don't take me to my car. I don't want to be alone. Take me to your place," she said huskily.

"I was hoping you'd say that," he whispered through a growing grin.

He drove to his house and pulled in the driveway. The moment he got out of the car he knew something was wrong. Lights were on in the house and the stereo system was blasting. They both pulled out their service weapons and crept towards the door. As he got closer he heard the song playing. "She Came in Through the Bathroom Window" thumped and pounded against the windows and door. They approached the door low and slow, each one flattening themselves on either side of it. Watson slipped his key in the door and twisted the knob. She went in to the left and he went in to the left to the left—first the smaller body, then the bigger one, so both could get an unobstructed view. The kitchen, living room, and dining room were clear, she called out. John slowly crept down the hall. The three bedroom doors were open. He checked each room and the closets. Last was the bathroom. He approached it slowly as the lyrics sang out.

And so I quit the police department
And got myself a steady job
And though she tried her best to help me
She could steal but she could not rob.

CHAPTER 23

Watson twisted the knob as Trew moved up beside him. He threw the door open and stared. It was obvious. Broken glass from the bathroom window was all over the floor. At his feet lay the lacerated, bloody body of Officer Marylee McCarren, still dressed in her uniform but now very much dead. Her body had been precisely placed, and a silver spoon jutted out of her mouth. He backed out of the bathroom, walked to the living room, and pushed the off button on his sound system. Then Watson pulled his phone from his pocket and called the station. Trew walked out of the bathroom and down the hall, her gun hanging at her side. Shock had drained the blood from her face. She dropped her body onto the couch next to him.

The two sat saying nothing, then Watson bent over and put his face in his hands. He muttered to himself, "I will get you, you friggin' bastard." By the time he straightened himself up, sirens were approaching the house. The crime scene investigation team would arrive soon after and begin their work.

Moses and Lopez arrived. Moses looked at Moondog and decided it wasn't a time for the two to talk about the killing or the crime scene. He simply said, "What can I do for you, Moondog?"

Watson shook his head from side to side, then called Lopez over. "Agent Trew left her car at the police station. Can you drive her back there to pick it up?" Trew protested. She wanted to stay with him. John put his hands on both of her shoulders and looked her in the eyes. "This is a cop killing, and that means even I have to step aside and let these people do their jobs. Give Lopez your statement back at the station, then go back to the hotel and rest. I will need you fresh tomorrow morning. We're going to catch the bastard, and I need you at full strength." He gave no other sign of affection. He released her body from his hands and Lopez walked out with her.

Watson turned back to Moses and gave him commands. "I want every inch of her body and uniform dusted, vacuumed, and photographed. This time he had to leave some clue." Moses instructed the investigation team to get it done and went back to his mentor. "Walk with me outside, Sammy. There are a few questions rolling around in my head, and I don't want any other ears to hear."

"Mole?" Moses asked.

Watson led him to the sidewalk in front of the house, then down a few houses before he began to speak. "Mole? Absolutely. Bungalow Bill knew Jean Gilson was being transferred. He knew that McCarren was a good detective, and that she was putting the pieces together. He knew that I would be out tonight. He knows way too much before I even know it." Watson stopped talking and raked his fingers through his graying hair before blowing out a breath. "I have an idea who is giving us away, and I have a few details that I need you to check. You report your findings to me and me alone," he said as he jerked his thumb back in his own direction.

The two headed towards the house. Moses asked, "Where are you staying tonight?"

"My brother's house. He was doing some research for me,

and it is time to find out what he has," John countered. They took a few more steps and Sammy stopped him by grabbing his arm.

"I forgot to tell you that one of your old drummers is in town," Moses said.

"Which one?"

"Dave Gettings. He came back for a funeral. I read about it in the paper."

"When did he get in?"

"The day before the first murder."

"Rather convenient."

"I thought so." Moses paused, then asked, "Should I go talk to him?"

"Yeah, absolutely. Do it in the morning, and invite him to the grand opening on Saturday night. I want to look in his eyes. Now, I'm going to head to my brother's house," Watson said as he pulled his keys from his pocket. He had turned to walk towards the car when he had another thought. "We will meet at ten in the morning to go over what I find out and what you find out. Just you and me and at the coffee shop."

He remoted his car door and climbed inside. Twenty minutes later he arrived at the old homestead, and saw only the lights on in his brother's office. He called to tell him he was at the door.

"You look bad, big brother. What happened?" Matt asked.

John gave the shortened version of the story, then asked, "What did you find?"

Matt ushered him into the kitchen and started a pot of coffee. As he was pouring in the water and coffee grounds he talked. "Jim McCall left town after high school. He did a few tours with the army. He was a sniper, and from his record, a good one. He moved back here to the Quads a few years ago after a divorce." Matt waited by the counter for the coffee to finish, and pulled two cups out of the cupboard. "No criminal record, but he did have some mental issues. It took me a few hours to hack the hospital, but it seems he is suffering from PTSD. He has person of interest written all over him." The coffee finished and Matt poured out two cups then sat down.

"What about Dave Gettings? The one I called about yesterday," John asked.

"He got into town the day before the killings started. He's been fairly successful in Chicago. His retirement papers are in and according to one article, he and his wife are moving to Florida at the end of the year. Nothing sinister in his background at all. No money laundering. No embezzlement. He is a clean government official."

John shook his head. "Does he have the money to have pulled all this off?"

"He does okay, but he isn't rolling in the dough. Unless there was embezzlement and no one ever caught it," Matt answered, then took a sip of the hot black coffee.

"Then we can't rule him out. He is here in town, and he does have a connection to Jean Gilson, to me, and the band. Check again for any funny money in his past." John paused and sipped his coffee.

"Next on your list was Walter 'Corky' Hodgdon. He ended up doing time for assault, then drifted out west. Not much was heard from him. No credit cards. No bank account. His name was thrown around as a person of interest in a shooting outside of Vegas about ten years ago, then he dropped off the radar again." Matt sipped his coffee and smiled a big smile. "Then, just about a week ago, he got a speeding ticket in Iowa City."

Watson smacked his hand on the table. "Well, how about

that! He looks like a person I need to talk to, but I have two problems with him." John held up one finger and said, "Jean Gilson said it wasn't him that she saw because of the cleft palate." Then Watson held up a second finger. "And two, Corky and I were good friends the whole time he lived down the street from here. He doesn't feel right to me." John took another sip. "He is worth a conversation though. See if you can get me an address or phone number."

Matt stood and motioned for his brother to follow him. They walked towards his office, and both took a seat with a view of the computer screen. Matt turned to John and said, "That leaves Jelly Jerry Jefferson. This one is a puzzle." Matt booted up the computer and entered Jefferson's search information. The early days came up quickly, but stopped two years after high school.

"Jefferson went to MIT. It turns out your friend Jelly was somewhat of a genius. Half way through MIT, he was thrown out of school. I hacked their computer system, but no records exist of his expulsion." Matt pointed to the screen. "At that point I picked up one reference to him in a newspaper out of Cambridge. He was arrested, but when I looked for that record, or any further records, or anything else, an error message came up." They both stared as Error ID 520 popped up on the screen. "Every search ends the same way with this message."

"What is Error ID 520? You know I know shit about computers," John questioned.

"It is a Data Protection Error message. Someone, somehow, has blocked all relevant information to Jerry Jefferson. He does not exist after his expulsion from MIT." Matt rolled his chair back from the desk. Looking directly at his brother, Matt confessed that he was completely confused.

"Could it be a government block?" John asked.

"No. The info would still exist, but I would get password protected sites then. He doesn't exist."

"Do you think he could be dead?" John asked as he stared closely at the error message while pushing his hair back from his forehead.

"There would be some record of that. His social security number isn't inactive. It has no known activity, but it doesn't list him as dead."

"It is suspicious then." Moondog stated as he sat straight in his chair. "A lot could be read into that fact, but it gives me nothing solid. Nothing to help me pinpoint his whereabouts or even his existence."

"I'd bet on this lead if it were actually a lead." Matt closed down the windows, and they both rose and walked back to the living room. Two steps into the room, John's phone rang.

"Watson," he answered. He listened and his expression soured. It wasn't good news, but obviously wasn't another killing. "Gotta run. Another clue was discovered, and they need me at the station." He shrugged on his sport coat and slouched out. He mumbled as he opened the door, "I hope I get some sleep tonight."

CHAPTER 24

Lopez was waiting for Moondog when he walked into the police station. "Let me hear it, Lopez."

"After they dusted for prints on the CD the investigators played the song, looking for any ambient noise or distinctive sounds. Nothing on that end, but what they found was a second song recorded on the disc. 'She Came In Through the Bathroom Window' was on a loop, so it was the only song that played." Lopez pressed the play button on the CD player.

"Golden Slumber/Carry That Weight/The End" was a medley by the Beatles that Johnny and the Moondogs had covered often over their years as a band. Bungalow Bill had taken the center song, "Carry That Weight," pulled it from between the two, and recorded it just for Moondog.

"Do you think it is a clue to the next killing?" Lopez asked as he pressed stop once the song finished.

Moondog shook his head from side to side. "No, that message was just for me. Gilson and McCarren were both direct messages to me. Their deaths were because of me. Bungalow Bill wants me to carry the weight of those deaths. They are retribution for whatever perceived injustice I have done to him." Moondog turned and headed to the door. "He wants me to carry the guilt, and the shame, and the responsibility for their cruel ends."

Watson scratched his head hard in frustration. His brain needed to wrap itself around all the clues and solve this murder spree. It had been a horrible day, and it needed to end. He turned and stepped out the door and headed to an old motel to get a good night's sleep. He needed it. The opening of Abbey Road was in two days, Ringo's concert was in three days, and Watson needed his mind sharp to catch the killer. He wasn't going to carry that weight. Or at least, that's what he thought until he was laying in the motel bed, lights off, and his exhausted mind and body crashed into a heavy sleep.

Faces—dead faces, alive faces, new faces, old faces, lots of faces—danced inside his dreams. He saw Jean Gilson, the Asian girl, the emaciated old man, Marylee McCarren, and all those that had fallen alongside them. They floated by. Then his dreams would take him back to his childhood. He saw the old band as they struggled to learn one song. Flashes of their first concert and the tremendous fear of being on stage. It was all running together, because it was together. Bungalow Bill was the other side of his life. It was another man obsessed with the lives of four men out of Liverpool. That obsession turned and twisted in an evil way.

In his dreams John chased clues, but each one fell down a rabbit hole. Each one was lost before it arrived. The killer would appear, but never his face. As the sunlight broke through the flimsy drapes in the motel room, a final image drifted in front of John's mind. It was Officer McCarren, sitting in the police station talking on the phone.

The dream was more than that. It was a lost memory; something was noticed, passed by, and never delivered, and never brought to fruition. He remembered words from her phone conversation—not sentences, not phrases, but a few words. He had heard Boston. Boston. Why was Boston important to McCarren? Boston. He heard Boston again in his head. Then he sat up straight in bed.

"She was getting close. That's why Bungalow Bill killed her. It wasn't about me. It was about her."

He snatched his phone from the nightstand and called Moses. Sam had gotten into the station early and picked up his phone.

"Moses, you need to find out what they did with McCarren's personal affects. After the fake call to the captain's office, a rookie was packing her stuff in a box. You have to find that box. There is something in it that could blow the lid off this thing," Watson rattled quickly as he raced to the shower.

"Will do," Moses responded.

When Watson arrived at the station he strode directly to Moses. "Where is the box?"

"Her father stopped in and picked it up," he reported.

"Does she even have a father? How do we know it was her dad? Who gave him the box? I want to talk to that person now."

Watson was flailing his arms and yelling. The captain walked out of his office when he heard the disturbance.

"I gave the man his daughter's things. I did it. So, what is all the yelling about, Watson? I'm the captain. I did it. So come in my office and talk to me about this horrible thing I did," the captain bellowed before turning back inside his small office. Watson stormed in behind him and slammed the door.

"Did you check his ID? Was it really her dad? Did you even know if she had a dad?" Watson blustered, with his anger right on the tip of his words.

"Slow down, John. Tell me what this is all about, and yes, it really was her dad. He is an old friend of mine. How do you think she got promoted so fast? He has her stuff. Now, tell me what this is about," the captain said as he dropped into his chair. Watson immediately calmed down and sat across from him. He explained the two clues that he had remembered. The one about the Massachusetts Institute of Technology, and the snippet of a phone interview by McCarren where she mentioned Boston. "There is a connection there, and McCarren was on to it. That's why she was killed."

"Her dad left here about thirty minutes ago. I'll call him and tell him to bring the box back. I kept her notebooks though," the captain said.

"She wasn't using a notebook. It was something else she was writing on. An envelope or a card of some type," Watson remembered.

"Then it will be in the box," the captain said. "You can search the box in an hour. Until then, stop the damn killer somehow."

John stood up and opened the door. The two men had been loud enough that most of the officers and detectives, along with Agent Trew, had heard the conversation. John felt a bit embarrassed by his overreaction. He quietly walked back to his desk and sat down. Moses and Trew took the two chairs across from him.

"Sorry you had to hear all that," he said in a subdued tone.

"Sammy told me what it was all about. Do you want me to run to McCarren's dad's house and pick up the box?" Trew asked. Her face was lined with concern.

John touched her hand. "No," he said as he patted her hand. "An hour will give me time to check out a few leads that have been rolling around in my head. Let me get to that." Watson pushed himself away from the desk between the three of them and stood. "We can look at the box when it returns." He walked away from the two.

Moses threw his arms up with his palms facing upwards.

"Sometimes I can't figure the guy out." He reached for a pencil and snapped it in two. His frustration with his boss was showing in subtle and not-so-subtle ways. Prudence smiled and nodded her head in agreement. She stood and headed to the door. As she exited she called back to Moses, "See you in an hour." His half smile was his goodbye.

Watson walked back to Moses briskly. "I changed my mind. Here's Mr. McCarren's address. Get there fast and grab the box. Use the lights, because I have a bad feeling that things could go poorly for the old guy if Bungalow Bill gets wind of the information. Go! No time for questions," Moondog instructed as he laid the scrap of paper on the desk. Moses was up and out the door immediately.

Mr. McCarren had stopped at the funeral home to help his wife with the arrangements for the viewing. He made it home just a minute before Detective Moses pulled behind him in the driveway. Moses got out and flashed his badge. "I'm Detective Moses, and if you don't mind, we realized that there might be an important note in the box about your daughter's killer. I'd like to pick it up and take it back to my office. I will return it tomorrow."

McCarren had been pulling the box off the back seat. He gave Moses a surprised look. "What could possibly be in here? It is just personal things," he responded before shrugging his shoulders and handing over the box. "If it can help find her killer then you can have anything you need."

Moses took the box, then said, "I want you to know that Marylee was good cop. She was a rising star, and will be a great loss to our team. You have my condolences." Moses nodded and tossed the box in his trunk. As he opened his front door to the vehicle, a black SUV cruised by slowly. The tinted glass kept Sammy from seeing the driver, but the slow speed set off alarms in his cop head. This was Bungalow Bill. He made a mental note of the license plate number and watched the vehicle pick up speed and drive away. He pulled his phone from his pocket and called Moondog.

"Watson here."

"John, you were right. I think I just beat the killer to McCarren. Run this plate and see if we can get a hit," Moses said, then repeated the numbers and letters from the plate.

"There is definitely something in that box. Get back here quickly and alive. I'm sending out some black and whites to escort you. We're onto this bastard," Moondog said excitedly.

Moses was already in his car and backing out of the driveway. "How did Bungalow Bill know? There is someone on the inside, if you want my opinion," Sammy snapped.

"I agree. We have a mole or moles, or there is some kind of secret surveillance inside the station. It doesn't matter what right now. We have to keep everything between just us. You and I, bud," Watson said as he hung up and called dispatch to send black and whites to intercept and escort Moses.

Sammy had the lights on and the siren blaring as he raced through the streets. As he crossed through one intersection, the black SUV skidded into position behind him from a side street. Hands came out of the SUV driver's side window and one out of the passenger's side window. Both held small automatic weapons, and both were firing as soon as they came out.

Bullets crashed into the rear window of Moses's unmarked car, shattering the glass and narrowly missing him. He kept his head down and once again dialed Moondog. "I've got two shooters in a black SUV behind me. I am taking shots. How long before the officers intercept me?"

John picked up his desk phone and called dispatch. He

was told five minutes. He got back on the phone with Moses. "You need to evade them for five minutes. The squad cars should intercept you. We have you on GPS, so do what you have to do."

Moses whipped the car into a side street then turned left again at the end of the block. The SUV hung with him. They gained distance and the guns appeared again, firing fast and accurately. He swerved from side to side to avoid the bullets, then punched the gas until he reached the next intersection. He hand braked into a slide then spun the wheel. The unmarked car skidded into the intersection then barreled straight ahead down the block. He did the same thing at the end of that block, and pulled onto the main drag headed for the police station. He swerved to avoid cars and sped away as fast as he could. The SUV made the turns then gunned the engine to catch up. Moses knew that up ahead was a stop light, and his chances of avoiding both an accident or a bullet to his head were slim, but he kept his pedal to the floor.

He was a hundred yards from the yellow light. It was stale, ready to turn. He needed to make a choice. He started to slow so he could avoid crossing traffic. The SUV caught up and he was in another hail of bullets. He felt wetness and pain in his shoulder. He was hit.

Suddenly two squad cars roared up behind the SUV. Bungalow Bill knew it was time to bail. He raced past Moses, who had ducked down as he came to a slow roll. Bullets broke his window and penetrated the passenger door. One squad car pursued the SUV and one pulled to a stop next to Moses, who had stopped. Seeing the blood, the officer radioed "Officer down," then pulled Moses from the car and dropped him into his backseat.

Watson came on the radio, "Grab the box."

"I don't see a box," the officer reported.

Moses yelled, "In the trunk."

The officer grabbed the box, dropped it on the front seat, and slid quickly into his car. He radioed that he was heading for the hospital when Moses stopped him. "It's not that bad. Take the box to the station and then take me to get patched up. That box is what this is all about."

The officer wanted to argue but followed orders. The other squad car followed the SUV for several blocks before it turned into an alley and disappeared.

Watson greeted Moses and the police officer as they pulled into the station parking area. He grabbed the box, looked at Moses, and said, "I can't believe you let yourself get shot."

Moses barked out, "Screw you."

They both smiled, and the officer took the detective to the emergency room.

CHAPTER 25

Watson dumped the contents of the box on the table in the task force room. He searched through every scrap of paper until he came upon an envelope from the police union. He flipped it over. Notes were scribbled across it. He tucked it into his pocket then tossed the contents back into the box.

Trew pushed the door open. She saw him with the box and walked quickly towards him. "Is what you were looking for in there?"

"Don't know. Moses just dropped it off and then went for a ride to the emergency room," he answered.

"What? What happened?" she exclaimed with concern and excitement.

"I believe it was Bungalow Bill that attacked him as he was driving back. He got me the box. Why don't you go through it while I check on my partner?" Moondog told her as he walked to the door, and then to his desk. She dumped the box out and went through it article by article, paper by paper, but found nothing. She sat and waited for him to return.

"I talked to Moses. He said he saw nothing but a black SUV and a shooter. The black and white lost the SUV after a few blocks. Did you find anything in the box?" Moondog asked.

"Not a thing. Do you think it was taken by the dad?"

"No, Moses caught him in the driveway, so he had no time to unpack it. It had to be my imagination or a bad memory.

Things are starting to run together. I need some rest before the grand opening tomorrow," he told her.

"Do you need company?" she asked with a sexy smile, filled once again with promise.

"No, I really need rest, and I have a feeling that rest isn't what's on your mind," he said as he picked up his keys and headed out.

She called after him, "How is Moses?"

"He'll live, and he better be back at work tomorrow," Moondog responded, then walked out the door.

Watson moved quickly to his car. He wanted to pull the envelope from his pocket and study it to decipher a clue or some bit of information, but instead he drove off. John had grown paranoid that his every move was monitored. As he pulled in front of his parent's homestead, John looked up at the house on the hill. He remembered the many times he had sat on that front set of steps, talking with friends and swapping dreams about what their lives would be like in the future. His life hadn't turned out the way his dreams had predicted. Right now, his dreams were more like nightmares. He needed to find Bungalow Bill and put an end to that killer's life, or at least his career.

John was still thinking about his dreams when he rapped on the door. His sister-in-law, Mel, answered quickly. She didn't smile as she saw him. Concern came over her face. "You look worse today than you did before. Come in and I will get you some coffee."

Mel pushed the door shut and walked to the kitchen. John took a seat on the couch and waited. His thoughts about dreams were fading as he pulled the envelope from his pocket.

It had notes all over it—snippets of ideas, words, information, and possible leads. He was still staring at it when

Mel placed a mug of black coffee on the table in front of him. "I'll let Matt know you're here," she said softly.

In a few minutes, John's youngest brother came down the old steps of the house. John recognized every creak of each step. Sixteen steps, he thought. Then his mind drifted back to the one nightmare that had haunted his childhood sleep. The dark, unknown figure at the top of the stairs. It motioned to him to climb towards it. It motioned for him to meet his fears at the top.

John was snapped out of his daydream by Matt's words. "Do we have something new?" the younger Watson said as he pointed down at the envelope.

"Yeah," John stated as he lifted the paper to Matt's reaching hand. "Detective McCarren was working on this when she was murdered. Right now, no one knows that I have it. No one but you."

"What about Moses?"

"He almost got killed retrieving it, but he is not aware of what is on it."

"What about that FBI agent?"

"No, that's the problem. She's a Fibbie, and that means that she can step in and take over at any time. I told you before, I don't like working with them because they are all take and no give." John moved his hands to his temples and rubbed. "She says she is on leave and is there to help. I believe her, but the FBI is still the FBI. They're the government."

"As Reagan said, 'I'm from the government and I'm here to help.' That is always a frightening scenario." Matt studied the notes. "The thoughts are a little disjointed. What have you gathered from them?"

John took a sip of coffee and settled in. Matt took the chair opposite him as John spoke. "Jelly Jefferson is dead. He died in a fire in Boston. Most likely he was cooking some kind of drug when it exploded. A corpse was found and dental records matched."

"So, your lead suspect is dead? Where does that leave you?"

"Back to nowhere," John said as he threw a fist at a pillow next to him.

"In my line of business, one set of facts leads to a new set of facts. Did you see this note scratched at the bottom? It says missing persons. That is another clue. Computer forensics is about more than money and bank accounts. Although, Jelly Jefferson's death would mean money was transferred to someone." Matt stood. "Let me dig a bit further and see what we have here." He turned towards his office door then spun around. "Does anybody know about me?"

"I suppose that since you were with me when I went to the cemetery, then Bill knows of your existence. And if Bill is an old acquaintance of mine he would know about you, and Eddie and Chris. He would know about you, yes."

"Should I be careful?" Matt asked with a tinge of fear in his voice.

"Yes," John said as he realized that he had put his own brother in danger. "I'm going to put an unmarked car outside your house at all hours. Try to keep Mel out of the mall for the next few days."

"Are you crazy? Dillards is having a big sale. She wouldn't miss that for anything."

"Then go with her."

"I would rather face Bungalow Bill than the crowds at the mall," Matt said with a laugh, then added, "I will be careful, and I will go with her."

John smiled as he exited and trudged down the cement

steps to his car. Matt had made him think. Maybe Jelly didn't die. Maybe he faked his own death to avoid an arrest. If so, who was he now? Bungalow Bill? Hey, Bungalow Bill, who did you kill, Bungalow Bill?

Chapter 26

His Cuban-heel boots echoed in the old church building as he strolled down the main aisle, pulling the lifeless body of Eleanor Rigby by her hair. The old churches doors were locked; the scent of Pontifical incense hung heavily in the air.

Bungalow Bill climbed the three marble steps to the sanctuary. The dead body bounced up each step and then slid easily to the altar. Bill used his whole arm to swipe the items from the altar onto the marble floor. The noise of the breaking altar pieces was ear shattering in the echoing walls and high ceilings.

He lifted the corpse onto the altar, neatly spreading her body lengthwise. "Eleanor, you did die in the church. We got that part right, didn't we? Now for the yucky part. Old Paulie wrote that you kept your face in a jar by that big wooden door. If I was a squeamish person, I might have to close my eyes and cut it off. But, to be quite honest, I do, do, do enjoy my labors. To me, you are a work of art. You may even be my best piece ever."

Bungalow Bill removed a leather wrapped packet from his pocket and selected his sharpest scalpel, then set to work slicing the face from the dead woman's head. Since her heart had already stopped beating, no spurts of blood splattered him. Instead, it seeped from the cuts onto the altar like a lifeless sacrificial lamb. As he sliced, he whistled the tune of "Eleanor Rigby" softly to himself through his smiling lips.

Once he finished, he wiped the scalpel, rolled it back into the leather holder, and placed that back in his pocket. With his bloody gloves he picked up the face and walked towards the front door of the church. Small droplets of blood fell from the face, leaving a faint trail from the altar to the jar. Bill didn't want old Johnny to miss his sly little play on the lyrics from the song. There, next to the aspersorium that held the holy water, was a large decorative jar. It had been donated weeks before by a wealthy, anonymous member. Bungalow Bill bent over and popped the lid from the jar. Holding the layer of facial flesh over the opening, he opened his fingers and dropped it in. Then he carefully moved the facial features until they were staring upward through the empty eye holes.

Bungalow Bill raised his head to get the full view. He grimaced. "You aren't smiling, Eleanor. If you smiled then maybe, just maybe, your smile would be as famous as Mona Lisa. Or if you grimaced, you could be Moaning Lisa." He paused, tilting his head from one side and then to the other. "I like the smile better." Bungalow Bill reached into the hand-painted jar covered with religious scenes, and pushed the corners of her mouth into a smile. He stood straight, placed the top back on the jar, and turned to walk away.

Bungalow Bill eyed the basin of holy water, and grinned again. A whimsical glint lit his eyes. Bill took two strides towards the basin and dipped his fingers into the holy water. A hissing sound was heard. He screamed in pain, recoiling his twisted fingers, and stared at them with mock horror. Then he laughed. "That one makes me laugh every time."

Giggles were developing in the back of his throat. They would soon be uncontrollable. He quickly ran to the back pew and dropped onto the red velvet cushion. The giggles had grown into snorts, and finally into full belly laughs.

Bungalow Bill laughed at his own sense of macabre humor. He spurted out a tune. "Kept her face in a jar by the—" Then the laughter came again and it was uncontrolled. His shaking hand reached for the kneeler and pulled it open, then he dropped both knees onto the hard, wooden support. He was buckling over with laughter as he draped his shoulders and head over the back of the pew in front of him. A few minutes passed. Bill was pulling in deep breaths to calm himself. He was finally able to pull himself to his feet once again and moved towards the altar. The maniac pulled his phone from his pocket and shot several pictures of the altar. He pulled up his email program and sent them to the Quad Cities Times.

He picked up his garbage bag to dispose of his gloves and walked to the front door. He twisted the lid of the jar and took more pictures. "Bye-bye, Eleanor," he said, then blew her a kiss. He opened the door, went down the marble steps, and walked into the darkness, singing to himself, "All the lonely people, who has killed them all." Soon his skipping, gyrating figure disappeared into the dark. It was 2 a.m., and it was time to wake up Moondog.

John "Moondog" Watson had finally fallen asleep after a fitful attempt. His dreams were unsettling. His visit to his childhood home had kicked the old scene of the man at the top of the staircase sharp into his unconscious mind. Once again the man was at the top of the stairs. Once again his features were hidden by the dark, and once again he motioned for John to climb the stairs. Always afraid, he had never gone. Always afraid, his voice was unable to call out to his parents. Always afraid until this night, until this dream. He took a step, then another. Sixteen steps to the top. Fourteen to go. He took two more, then two more. He was halfway there, and the figure continued to motion him to climb. Trance like, Watson moved up two more, then two more. The figure raised his face. The light from the living room shed enough ambient glow that John could almost recognize the face.

His cell phone rang. "Watson here." Then the eerie music of the song "Eleanor Rigby" floated from the phone's speaker. His body broke out in a sweat. Bungalow Bill had struck again.

Watson pushed his speed dial for Moses. "Can't a guy take a day off after getting shot?" Moses said into his phone.

"Bungalow Bill struck again. Meet me at the station. We don't have a location, only a lead," Watson reported. Agitation mixed with frustration came through the line.

"I'll be there, boss," Moses stated, and got off the line.

Watson's next call was to Trew. He needed her expertise on the Beatles. He no longer trusted just his brain to figure out the clues. "Bungalow Bill struck again."

"What was the clue? What was the song?" she asked.

"'Eleanor Rigby,'" he answered.

"Gotta be a church somewhere. I'll review the lyrics on the way in, and I'll pick up coffee. Who else is coming?" she said. There was no sleep in her voice. Watson assumed she had been up already.

"Just Moses," was the short answer.

"He's been shot. Why are you dragging him into this one? We can handle it ourselves," Trew expressed virulently.

"'Cause I can trust him to get done what needs to be done. Nobody gets a day off until this Bungalow bastard is locked in a cage."

"I will be there in about forty-five minutes," Prudence stated, then hung up.

When Watson and Moses entered the task force room, Trew was already there with three coffees, her computer open and the lyrics for "Eleanor Rigby" printed out. She was standing with both palms on the table, spread on either side of the paper in front of her. She raised one hand to her hair as it hung in her face and pushed it back behind her ear. Smiling, she said, "Good morning. According to John and Paul's lyrics, Eleanor died in a church, she was lonely, she was forgotten, she had picked up rice after a wedding, and kept her face in a jar by the door."

"That last one doesn't sound good," Moses mumbled as he grabbed a Styrofoam cup of coffee and blew on the open contents to cool them.

"Put the picture together, Trew. I think you already have ideas," John instructed.

"We are probably looking for an old, large church building, and if the rice is a clue, then one that had a recent wedding or has one later this morning," Trew said as she slipped into her chair and sipped from her cup.

Moses sat across from her. "I know nothing about churches in the area. I can't be much help there. Although, this guy is making me believe that the devil is alive and well and living in the Quad Cities. If he is, then I better get myself back to church."

"The three oldest, largest churches are St. Marks, St. Johns, and St. Marys. St. Johns would be a good bet because it has my name, but St. Marys is where I went as a kid. In fact, my earliest band played one of the CCD dances a long time ago," he added. "Of course, we played St. Johns as well."

Trew tapped away at the keys on her computer. "I'm checking to see who just got married and who is getting married later today. That might narrow it down some more." She paused and waited for the websites to fill in the screen. "This doesn't help. All three have weddings tomorrow. None had weddings today." She continued to search.

Growing impatient, Watson directed his order towards Moses. "Call dispatch and have black and whites go to all three locations. I want to know if there is anything unusual."

Moses rose gingerly and walked towards his desk, where he ordered the checks on all three churches. When he walked back in, Agent Trew was sitting back in her chair running her fingers through her hair while mumbling obscenities. She raised her eyes towards Moses and spat out, "Damn thing froze."

They all waited for the computer to reboot, saying nothing. They sipped coffee and dealt with the frustrating delay. When the computer was back online, Trew went back to searching the three church websites one at a time. She mumbled, "Nah," twice before hitting onto something. "This is it. St. Marys! Listen to this. 'For questions regarding facility rental for weddings contact Eleanor Robinson.' That's the one!" she said as she punched her finger into the computer screen. Moses jumped up to call dispatch and she added, "Make sure they approach with extreme caution."

Moses nodded his head. By the time he finished the call, the three were racing towards Watson's car.

***

The officers approached the half open front door of St. Marys church. They pushed it open and entered one low and one high, one to the left and one to the right, guns out and ready. The lights were dim in the vestibule. The two pushed open every door to closets and stairways. Finding nothing, they moved to a dark area under an overhanging balcony. The two were apprehensive about what might be lurking above them on the balcony. They separated and approached the open pews from the two ends, both watching the balcony. It was clear. The two moved to the confessionals, opening each door for a quick search. Both sets of eyes moved to the sanctuary at the front of the church, and fell upon the female form lying dead across the blood-stained, white marble altar. At that moment, they both heard steps in the vestibule. They spun and readied their weapons. Both were tense, and neither wanted to die the way the woman on the altar had died.

***

"Stand down, officers. Detective Watson here. What have you found?" John yelled as they entered. Moses and Trew were on his heels as he approached the two officers near the altar. As he climbed the three marble steps to the sanctuary, Trew moved to his side.

"It is exactly what I suspected," she whispered. John looked down at the corpse as he moved closer. The face had been removed. "Her face that she keeps in a jar by the door," she added.

Watson slowing moved his head to look at Moses. "Sammy, check to see if there is a jar by the door."

"Yeah, send Moses to look at the spooky, dead face peeking out from a jar. Let Moses get the shit scared of him," Sam remarked. He was half kidding and half not. Bungalow Bill's penchant for the macabre was finally overwhelming his sensibilities.

Once in the vestibule, he looked around for a jar and saw a large, ornate urn. Putting on latex gloves and pulling a pen from his pocket, he slipped it inside the loop on the top of the lid and lifted. Staring back at him was a nose, with two eye holes and a grin surrounding it. It was a face, and it was kept in a jar by the door. "Yep, it is in here." Only his years on the force kept him from throwing up his last meal.

Watson turned to the officers and instructed them to stay and secure the scene. The crime investigation team would be there soon. Then turning to Trew, Watson said, "I am tired of this guy always being ahead of us. I want you and I to sit down, go over Beatles songs, and look for the ones that have potential for being the next killing. We need to get out in front of him. We need to get way out ahead of him."

"I agree," she answered.

Moses, Trew, and Watson drove back to the station. Sammy told them he was going home to rest before the grand opening of Abbey Road that night. He advised John and Prudence to do the same thing, but they didn't.

Once in the room sitting across from one another, Agent Trew printed out two complete lists of all the Beatles songs. "You go through your list and circle every one that you think has potential. I will do the same. That way we can narrow it down to the ones we both think are likely."

Over the next half hour, the two circled their potential crime clues. Then they compared and eliminated, therefore forming a shorter list. Trew compiled the compared list on one page and printed it out. The two started at the top to sort out the possibilities. She started the conversation.

"What about 'Get Back'? Lots of city and name references in the song," she suggested. "There is the name Loretta Martin, who is obviously a transgendered person. Is there a gay bar in the Quads where transgenders go?"

"Connections. That is a possibility. Put a check next to that one," Moondog said. "'Happiness is a Warm Gun' is ripe with potential. I actually suspected that one a lot earlier. Maybe it is too obvious."

She grinned. "You're right. He hasn't been too obvious yet. Do any of these songs tie into your life at all? I mean, he seems to have you on his target list."

John pushed away from the table and paced while looking

at the list in his hand. He said nothing. After two minutes he smacked the paper with the back of his knuckles and blurted out, "'I Am the Walrus' mentions pigs several times, but I can't tie the walrus or the egg man to anything. I thought I had a good one, but on second glance it doesn't make sense." He paced some more, then threw out, "'Octopus's Garden' is a possibility. We do live next to the mighty Mississippi River. It could be the location of victim."

"Impossible to stake out the entire river," Prudence responded.

"Good point. What about 'Rocky Raccoon'? It is a story song. I think it is worth some examination." Trew paused, tapped a few keys, and the lyrics came up on her screen. "We have Rocky, Dan who stole his girl Magil, who called herself Lil—"

Moondog interrupted. "And everyone knew her as Nancy. I can see the setting now—a country and western bar, a lovers' triangle, and gunshots. That is a real good maybe if this was a country and western movie. We'll have Lopez look into that one, but I don't think it will pan out."

Trew grinned up at him. "We both liked 'Run for Life,' which is pretty obvious. How does he pull that one off, though? Does he chase a girl while playing the song? Once again there is no place to stake out." Trew sat back and folded her arms. "I feel like we aren't getting into his head. We have to think like he does."

"That's what profilers do, isn't it?"

"But I feel like I'm too close to this one. Someone I care about is the main focus of this killer and I am not thinking clear. Look at the next title on the list, 'Sexy Sadie.' We need to attach that biography or name to a local character, but I don't have any knowledge of local characters. Do these towns have anyone who could fit the description?"

Moondog shook his head no. There was no Sadie that turned everyone's head presently, but way back in high school there was Sherrie. Sherrie had followed the band around, from their early Daydreamer days. She was younger than the boys in the band. It was obvious that when she grew up she would be a beautiful woman, but at that time she was just Sherrie, the little kid that followed the band. The years were both good and bad to her. She had developed into a very beautiful girl. By then the band was Johnny and the Moondogs, and she wanted the lead Moondog.

John remembered the night when the band had started to play the song "Sexy Sadie" during one of their appearances, then out of the crowd slinked Sherrie. She was in a short, short mini-skirt and a low-cut, tight, pink top that proved to all around her that she had grown-up. As he sang the lyrics to the song, Sherrie danced, very suggestively, in front of him. John couldn't take his eyes off her, and she knew it. She teased his young libido unmercifully.

As the song ended, she sauntered back through the crowd. John was speechless. He stood motionless and stared. As she reached the end of the crowd, she turned, smiled, and blew him a kiss. John had been ready to toss his guitar down and run after her when Jimmy, the bass player, grabbed his arm and whispered, "Don't do it, Moondog. She is bad news now. Let's move on to the next song." They did.

From that point on, Sherrie had the nickname Sexy Sadie. Jimmy was right, she was bad news. Lives and marriages were ruined over her. There really was a Sexy Sadie in his life, but it had been a long time ago. She had left town for college, and as far as he knew, had never returned.

"Moondog, are you still with me?" Trew asked.

"Yeah, just feeling a little weary, and we have big night ahead of us."

"Do you want to stop or do you want to go back to your house to finish, and let you rest?"

He turned her way and grinned. "I don't think we'll rest if we go back there. Let's finish these up, and then I have to get to Abbey Road to check on the progress of preparations." He sat across from her and they started discussing the songs again.

"'Let It Be' is a possibility. I will listen to the song while you're at Abbey Road and see if there is anything that comes to mind," Prudence said. Trew gathered up her computer, and as she placed it in the bag she looked up at Moondog. "What time do you want me at Abbey Road?"

"The grand opening starts at seven, so come early so you can be by my side all night," Moondog answered.

"All night? Now who's flirting?" she said with a flashing smile, then licked her lips. "Can't wait for the all night part." She snatched up her bag and headed for the door. Her hips seemed to have a little more swing in them, and John watched every swing.

Once she left he grabbed the list he had originally circled from the garbage can. He wanted to know which songs she had eliminated from his list. That was precisely where he would begin.

CHAPTER 27

After checking on the grand opening preparations, Moondog stepped into his office with the owner of the security company he had hired for the evening. They went over the dozen new surveillance cameras that were added, and the digital recording equipment. Any corner or nook that could not be accessed by camera was accessed by wireless microphones. Every detail would be recorded. Watson knew that Bungalow Bill would be there just to taunt him, by touching shoulders and then walking out unfounded.

Each glass being used that evening had a visible but decorative marker placed on it. After the event every glass would be dusted for prints, and every print run through a database. No one knew of this preparation. No one would know until the party was over. Security men and women would be serving drinks and filling the hors d'oeuvres trays. They would also clandestinely scan each person for bugging devices, guns, or explosives. Moondog wanted nothing to get by him.

Thirty minutes before the doors would open, Prudence Trew showed up at the door and knocked. Moondog beamed at her while opening the door. "You look fantastic," he commented on her tight, simple black dress. Her brunette hair fell across her shoulders, framing her face with the dark waves.

"I am here to be by your side, just like you asked,"

Prudence responded. "And by it I will stick."

"No complaints from me. Can I get you something to drink?"

"Just water. I am on duty tonight, as your bodyguard, and maybe a little more," she answered, then grinned sexily his way. "That is, until the all night part starts. Then you'll need a real body guard to keep me from what I am thinking inside my little head."

"I gave the body guard the night off. I will have to protect myself but, I must admit, I am a lousy guard," he said. "Let me introduce you to the band."

The two walked over to the small stage, where Moondog and Trew spoke with each member. He excused himself, leaving her to chat with his old friends. John looked up to see Moses pushing the door open while carrying a large suitcase with his good arm. The two entered the office.

"Do you really think you'll need to dust every glass?" Moses asked as he placed the case on the floor.

Watson looked him in the eyes and nodded his head yes. "Bill will be here tonight. We're going to make sure that we get an idea of who he really is. He's been too careful, but no one can get away with wearing gloves to a store opening. If someone comes in wearing gloves then arrest him. Got it?" Watson expressed.

Moses shrugged. He had learned to follow his mentor's lead. Watson looked at his watch and pulled the office door open. Grabbing the man assigned to door security, he moved to the door. The guard took his position and John opened the door to let in his early guests. With the door wide open, guests and well-wishers filed into the store. John greeted each one. Most he knew. His brother Matt, his sister-in-law Mel, his brother, Eddie and his wife, Andrea, several more relatives, police officers and their wives, and then the mayor came to the door.

"Mr. Mayor, thank you for this honor," John said as he grabbed the mayor's arm and hand with both of his hands.

"Geesh Lousie, Moonie, don't lay on the crap. You and I closed down way too many bars together back in the day," the mayor said as he put his arms around his old friend. The mayor's wife, an old girlfriend of Moondog's, gave him a big embrace.

"Here's the one I shouldn't have let get away," Moondog said as his eyes rolled up and down on the mayor's wife. She smiled. She had turned into a wonderful lady and a good friend over the years. "I see that you're running for mayor again this year. You can count on my support."

"We've done a good job, but I feel that the area still needs to come together to accomplish a lot more. In fact, that's my motto: Come Together! Like it?" the mayor said.

Watson logged that comment away. He didn't like it, not in the light of all that was going on with Bungalow Bill.

Behind the mayor was a familiar face, but John couldn't place it. Then it struck him. "David Gettings! Is that really you?"

"Yep, old buddy, it's me," David answered as he took Moondog's hand and shook hard.

"I never expected you. What brings you to town?"

"My uncle died, and my mom is ill. You remember her, don't you?" David asked.

"Yes, yes, yes. The poor woman put up with our horrible little band practicing in her dining room. She was an absolute saint for that alone. We were so terrible back then. It had to have been our drummer. He was horrid," Moondog joked.

"That drummer was great. It was the vocalist that was

bad," David retorted, and then hugged John again. "We had such a good time back then. Thanks for making a year of my life fun. People at my office can't believe I ever did anything that normal. An accountant is just not good rock 'n' roll material." David looked behind him to see a line forming. "I better get out of your way. Maybe we can get together before I have to leave and go back to Chicago."

Moondog, still with a grin on his face, said, "Sure." He then turned to the others entering. After listening to Moondog's earpiece, Moses walked out of John's office and caught Gettings. Sammy had Gettings on his list of potential suspects. He was going to make sure that they met and set up a time for further questioning.

John was needed near the stage area and left the door. More people crowded into the store, grabbed drinks and food, looking around at the memorabilia, and laughing about the LPs that they used to have. An hour later, as the filled room vibrated with conversation and few new people strolled in, Trew whispered in Moondog's ear that she was slipping outside for fresh air. As she re-entered, Moondog saw her walk a few steps ahead of a tall, thin man that he didn't recognize.

The man was by himself and seemed to be quite interested in the items on display. He walked around and grabbed a glass of champagne. Moondog was curious. He moved next to Moses and whispered that he wanted the man's print taken as soon as possible. Any new face would be suspicious to Watson—any new one, at all. He looked back over the crowd. There were several more unknown faces. He wanted them all. He was tempted to arrest every new face and deal with the fall-out later on. He was ready to do that when one of them pushed his way through the crowd towards him.

He extended his hand and said, "I'm Louis Clark with the

Times. I want to do an interview with you. I think this is great for the city, especially since we have some maniac terrorist running around. Do you have any leads on that one?"

"Sorry, I don't comment on on-going investigations. Besides, I am in pre-retirement mode. I am not that much involved with cases right now. My focus is on Abbey Road and my life after the police force," Watson answered.

"I can understand that, but this case has gotten a lot of attention. Things like this don't happen in the Quad Cities. Why would a terrorist attack people in our town? Like the judge and the two women at the courthouse. That elderly teacher would be another questionable terrorist attack. This morning the newspaper got photos of a murder victim laying on the altar at St. Mary's church. Her face had been removed, and placed in what looked like a large jar. These don't have the earmarks of a terrorist attack. It seems more like serial killer to me. And from eyewitness accounts you are pretty well knees deep in this whole investigation." Clark pressed hard before his final appeal. "So, how about an interview?" Clark requested.

Watson sighed. This was a moment he wasn't looking forward to. "Tell you what. Once the investigation is over, I will sit down with you and give you everything. I mean everything. You could do a damn book from what I will tell you. It will be an exclusive. I just can't talk about anything right now. Fair enough?"

"Is that the best you can give me?" Clark pushed back.

"At this point in time, yes. Now, you will have to excuse me. The Moondogs are already on stage, and that means I need to be there, too."

John pushed past the reporter towards the stage. Trew moved up beside him, tugged his face towards her, and kissed him. He smiled in return.

Jimmy moved next to him as he threw his guitar strap over his head. "Who is the new Sexy Sadie? To be honest, she looks a like the original Sexy Sadie."

"An FBI agent that wants to investigate my body," John smirked. Jimmy laughed and moved into position.

John "Moondog" Watson stepped to the microphone. "It is wonderful to see all these friends and family, and so many potential new friends. Although we are here to celebrate the grand opening of my new store, Abbey Road, I feel like I need to thank the world's greatest rock 'n' roll group, the Beatles, for giving us all decades of great music. For those of us in America, it all started with this song."

John struck the first chord of "I Want to Hold Your Hand" and the band ran through their usual opening set. "A great change came to the music world when the Beatles decided to make the first concept studio album. It was Paul's idea to create a completely new identity for the group. This was the song that kicked it all off."

As the band prepared for the number, three men walked into the room; two of them large with roaming, studious eyes, and a third who was much smaller, bearded, and wearing sunglasses. John immediately knew who it was. His brain could not believe what his eyes were seeing.

When the Moondogs hit the first note of "Sgt. Pepper's Lonely Hearts Club Band," the smaller man's face snapped up to look at the band. His well-known, sneering grin shot across his face, and he moved quickly towards the stage.

As the band ended the song, the man climbed on the stage with them. "If you're playin' me song then I'm singing it." The room went quiet. No one had any doubt as to the identity of the man on-stage. Moondog shrugged his shoulders and smiled with a happiness that he hadn't shown in years. He nodded to the others and started their lead in to "With a Little Help from My Friends." As the song ended the crowd broke into whistles and cheers. The famous drummer took an exaggerated bow, then turned to Moondog, shook his hand, and said, "When I read about this in the paper, I knew I had to come. I didn't expect to have a chance to say thanks in that way."

John's face flushed as he spoke. "It is me who needs to say thanks for all the years of getting to play your great music, and you joining in will be a memory I will never forget. Thank you." The famous drummer did a thumbs up to the rest of the band and stepped off the stage. His bodyguards kept people from mobbing him, but he gladly signed any object placed in front of him.

"How can I top that one?" Moondog said into the microphone. "Our next number is a special message for someone in the room. You know who you are."

***

The band started into "The Continuing Story of Bungalow Bill." Several heads snapped back to the stage. Moses watched on camera to see the expressions on the unknowns. No one gave anything away, but he knew it was registering in someone's mind as Moondog moved through the lyrics. Two of the unknown men moved closer to the door. Moses moved out of the office towards the door as well. He wanted to watch them both up close and personal. Both of them noticed him. They looked towards the door and saw two large security people blocking the exit. One of the men slipped back into the crowd. The other stood grinning until Moondog started the second song in their short set—"I'll Get You." On the first note, the man moved quickly into the crowd. Moses lost

143

track of him. He knew it was the first man who had walked in behind Trew earlier in the evening.

The elusive stranger was lost in the small but dense crowd. Moses grabbed Lopez, who stood at the back of the store. They both cut through the crowd searching for the thin, dark haired man. Sammy spoke into his mouthpiece, warning the two guards by the door to not let anyone out. He gave the description of the one they were looking for.

"Detective Moses, the only one that left was a woman. She appeared ill, so we let her out to get some fresh air," came the response.

Sammy and Lopez continued searching through the crowd. When Moondog ended the song and the set, the crowd thinned and moved towards the refreshments. It was then that Moses saw the black suit lying on the floor. He knew that the ill woman had been Bungalow Bill making his escape. The killer had expected a trap and prepared an escape. It had worked, and Moses was left holding an empty suit. He looked at Watson, still on stage, and shook his head from side to side. The head detective stepped down from the stage towards Moses.

"Did we get prints from him?" he asked.

Sam answered, "Yes."

"Run them immediately. Bag his glass for DNA, and get the suit to the lab as well. We finally have something on this guy," he snapped.

Trew joined the group. She stared at the suit and asked, "Bill's?"

"It appears so," Moses answered.

"How did he get away? I thought we had a tight perimeter," she questioned.

"So did I," Watson answered. "Something tells me he was

ready for every one of our moves. He knows what we know before we even know it. He's got inside help." Watson let out a breath and turned to the other two. "The show must go on. I need to mingle with the guests. Send Lopez back to the station with the suit and glass. Sammy, run those prints. Tell me everything as soon as you know it."

Watson looked over at his official Beatles guest, who was still signing autographs on the memorabilia. It would be a good night of sales for Abbey Road, as people purchased the freshly signed items from the frantic, overworked clerk at the register.

John pushed his way towards the drummer and shook his hand once again. He thanked him for singing and for coming. Along with the bodyguards, they walked towards the exit. The famous drummer waved to the crowd, called out a goodnight to everyone, then walked into the evening air. Watson thought it had been a very good night and a very bad night.

CHAPTER 28

The crowd thinned around ten that night. Business had been good, and it was evident that the many people who attended would talk about the evening for a long time. John caught up with David Gettings, his old drummer, and pulled him into his office.

"I need to talk to you, David. I need you to go way back in your memories and think about the original band. When you left the group, did you feel any animosity towards me?" Watson said as he sat on his desk and offered David a seat.

"Not at all. If I did I wouldn't have come tonight to see you. Boy, I am glad I did. Can you believe who sang that song with you?" David exclaimed. His excitement was genuine.

"Can you remember anyone else that might have a vendetta against me? What about Corky, or John McCall?" Watson probed.

"Corky left town before junior high, and John McCall.... Well, didn't he hang out with Billy Houk? You should ask Billy about him." David paused and thought for a moment. "What about the drummer that replaced me when the group became Johnny and the Moondogs? I don't remember his name, but I do remember him talking trash to me about the band back in high school. What was his name?" David asked as he scratched the air, trying to recall it.

"Jelly Jerry Jefferson," John said, filling in the memory blank for his old friend.

146

"He did not like you. That's for damn sure." David stopped, then narrowed his eyes looking at John. "That's what all these killings are about, isn't it?"

"That's what I think, but I can't prove it," John responded as he stood. He grabbed a file from his desk and showed David the old classroom picture from when they were kids. "Does anyone else strike you as someone who could do these killings?"

"It's been so long, Johnny. I'm lucky I remember the names of the people in my office every day. I haven't seen Jelly since the last day of school, when he spray painted your car," David said.

"That was him? That bastard. I'd shoot him just for doing that," Watson said, then leaned in closer. "Did you see him do it?"

"No, that girl you guys called Sexy Sadie was with him, and I saw her throw the can of spray paint in the garbage can outside of the high school on graduation day."

"Did you ever see her again?" John asked.

"Rumor was that she got pregnant and ran off with someone. The only one I ever saw her with was Jelly. I went off to college and lost track of everyone. Mom sent me all the newspapers, but I ran out of time to read them. Don't know more than that. Sorry," David told him with an apologetic shrug. He stood, and the two embraced and walked out of the office together.

John looked around. Most of the crowd had left. Moses was packing up the forensic equipment while Lopez helped. Lopez had run the suit to the police station and returned to help. He went into the office and pulled the hard drives with all the camera videos. On Monday morning they planned to review it all frame by frame. Sunday would be spent tightening security on the Ringo concert at the iWireless Center.

As the last person exited, Prudence Trew slithered up next to Moondog. She touched his arm and softly and sexily said, "Is it the all night part yet?"

He smiled at her. "Absolutely."

"I've never slept with a rock star before. That is, if you don't count Rod Stewart, Mick Jagger, and a few of the others." She laughed at her own joke.

"I can't imagine anyone turning you down. I'm not, that's for sure." He grabbed her hand and pulled her towards the front door. "Let's go back to my big, rock star mansion, and you can tell me how good I was tonight."

"I'll save that for an hour from now," Trew laughed.

"Better save it for two or three hours. I am a man of experience." He locked up and they both drove back to his house.

Two hours later, as promised, Prudence purred in his ear how good he had been that night. She cuddled up close and laid her head on his chest. He felt her head turn slightly to look at him. "Was that old drummer friend of yours able to shed any light on the case?"

"Nope. It was nice to see him, but he was no help to our investigation at all. What was your take on him?" John asked. He was exhausted, but he wanted to know what she thought.

"I thought he was odd. He kept looking at me like he knew me, or maybe that he wanted to know me. Men are like that," she said in a low tone. "I think you need to keep him on your persons of interest list. Something about him bothered me."

Trew yawned. Watson yawned. The next thing they remembered was the alarm going off on Sunday morning.

CHAPTER 29

Watson drove to the iWireless Center around noon. He wanted to assure himself that every detail of his security plan was in place. An actual Beatle would be a great temptation to Bungalow Bill. So far he had no song for a clue or as a challenge, but he expected it to come. His mind ran through every song that Ringo sang, and every hit he had after the Beatles separated. Nothing was moving forward in his brain. He had sung the greatest of his Beatles songs the night before. "With a Little Help From My Friends" could be the target song. "It Don't Come Easy" from his solo days might be the trigger song, but nothing struck Moondog as he walked the center. He checked every closet and every small nook in search of something that looked out of place. He knew that the one thing that would stop Bungalow Bill was vigilance. He had to watch and wait. That he planned to do.

As he walked through the concert hall he heard someone call his name. He turned to see Agent Prudence Trew, her face lit with a smile. It took all that both of them had inside them to keep it professional and not embrace.

"Anything out of the ordinary?"

"Not at all," he stated.

"I've been thinking about trigger songs," Trew stated as she stared around the cavernous room.

"Me, too."

"Ringo only sang eleven songs with the Beatles. A few

were monster hits. It could be only a few of those. I am guessing 'Yellow Submarine.'"

"What did you say in the beginning? He only sang eleven songs? That could be the trigger right there. It is trivia, and that seems to be one of the triggers for Bill," Watson said as he clapped his hands together.

"Eleven?" she queried.

"It's one more than ten. It goes to eleven," Watson said with a British accent.

Trew looked at him oddly. "I don't understand."

"Just a bad joke from an old movie called *Spinal Tap*," he remarked, and moved on quickly. It was the foible of dating a younger woman. "It could be the eleventh song in his set."

"That is exactly what I mean. It could be anything," she told him as she threw her arms in the air in frustration. "It could be anything," she said again, as in a whisper to herself.

"Let's talk to the manager and see if we can get his set of songs for the evening. We can target several possible trigger songs, and keep extra vigilant during those songs." Watson turned and headed to the man behind the sound board giving directions to the others. Watson flashed his badge as the two approached. The manager stepped away from the sound board and looked at them.

"How can I help?" he said.

"I am Detective Watson and this is Agent Trew of the FBI. All we need is the setlists for Ringo," he stated. John was trying to defer to the time constraints of the manager. The other man walked over to his seat and picked a folder up from the chair. He removed a sheet of paper and passed it to Watson.

"The All Stars are a big part of the show. Ringo does several of the Beatles hits and some of his own, but the All Stars are pretty big rock stars on their own. Wait until you hear them all on Gregg Rollie's 'Black Magic Woman.' Completely dope," the manager said.

John waved the setlist in the air and thanked the man for his help. He led Trew to the foyer away from the sound checks. "He does 'Yellow Submarine,' 'What Goes On,' and 'Matchbox' from the Beatles days. Which one strikes you as the one?" John asked as he fell into a chair in the foyer.

"All three. I think we need to concentrate on any song he did with the Beatles. Bungalow Bill hasn't used any of their solo songs." She paused. "As of yet." They both groaned at that thought and future possibility.

"Agreed. These are the ones we concentrate on. The other songs would have no message to us, and therefore are not right for Bill. I want to make copies of this list and get them to every officer and security guard. They need to crank up their vigilance at these intervals." They sat quietly, looking at the list as if it were going to speak actual words to them. Nothing came.

"I guess we wait," Trew finally said, pulling them both out of their own thoughts.

"Just like we've been doing. Tomorrow, if we don't catch him tonight, we will use our list of possible songs and cover all the bases with them. Until then, let's get something to eat." He stood and the two walked out of the center.

***

As they exited, neither noticed the caterer wheeling in heavy carts of food. The long legs on his thin frame strained hard to roll the carts up the ramp. He knocked on the side access door. A security guard opened it and helped to pull the cart inside. The two headed towards the dressing rooms. Once they turned right along the hall corner, the caterer pulled a long, thick metal pole from under the cloth covering the food.

He raised his arm and the blow came down hard on the head of the guard, who then collided with the floor.

The caterer pulled the guard into a closet, stripped the guard of his uniform, then pulled a Japanese, ceremonial sword from under the cloth on the cart. The caterer drew in a breath through grinning lips, and slit the man's throat. The blood splattered across the white catering uniform. The killer wiped his hands across the breast of his white jacket and peeled off the jacket and pants, bunching them under the cart's tablecloth cover. He changed into the guard's uniform. The caterer pushed the cart into the closet and locked the door before pulling it shut.

The security guard/caterer moved down the hall humming "With a Little Help from My Friends." He moved towards the office that held the security camera feeds to computer monitors. Pushing the door open, he looked inside. The man at the desk looked up at him and said, "You're the new guy they called me about, I take it?"

"Yep, I'm Pete Best. Nice to meet you. Where do you want me to post myself?" the fake security guard asked.

"Here's a map of the building. Familiarize yourself with the doors, the hallways, and the catwalks. Once you've covered the whole place come back here, and I will go over the night's assignments," the chief of security said as he rolled towards a desk and pulled a map from the top drawer. He handed it to the new guard.

"Lotsa cameras," the new man said. "Do we have eyes everywhere?"

"No frigging way," the chief said. "We are blind behind the stage and up high. Doors have cameras. The stage has cameras. The lobby has cameras. But that is about it," the chief said as he pointed to the monitors to his one side. "We use guards like you to cover those areas. Now, go and get the lay of the land. We meet back here at six to get our assignments and instructions for the night." The chief swung his chair around and went back to his cameras.

As the new security guard was winding through the hallways, the door he had originally entered buzzed. The chief came on his radio and asked the new guard to open the door for the caterers. He could only smile at his own timing of getting there first, using the caterers as a ruse. He smiled and opened the door to let them in. Then he continued to move along the hall, locating every camera and every visual dead spot. Once his reconnaissance was over, he moved back to the closet where the dead original guard lay, pulling a large case from under the cloth on his cart. He once again locked the door and exited down the hall with his case, heading for the steps to the catwalks.

In the darkness, he assembled his sniper rifle and hid it safely. Using binoculars, he located the center stage and the roadie setting up the microphone. He had a clear view and a clear kill shot. Now, it was time to wait. The guard guided himself along the catwalk, softly singing "Yellow Submarine." He stopped as Ringo and the All Stars came out for their sound check. He looked down at the rock stars below him and raised his hand, forming it into a gun. He dropped his thumb as if it were the pistol's hammer. His mouth twisted into a smile as he said, "Incoming torpedo."

He climbed down from the catwalk, casually walked to the backstage area, and stood watching the sound check. As the All Stars and Ringo exited, he smiled at the all of the stars for the night. Once Ringo passed, he said softly to himself, "Replace me, huh, Johnny? You'll pay for that move, and so will this replacement."

,

CHAPTER 30

That evening John and Trew watched the VIP's of the Quad Cities come streaming into the iWireless Center for the charity event. Finger foods were set in the foyer, and champagne moved throughout the crowd in trays carried by waiters and waitresses. John wore his one and only tuxedo. He thought he looked like the Sean Connery version of James Bond in his classically styled formal wear. Trew moved next to him and wrapped her arm around him. He waited for a compliment.

"Could Bungalow Bill be one of the waiters?" Her question deflated his aging ego, but her arm felt good.

"Thought about it. Before you came I watched each waiter check in with the caterer. None of them fit the physical profile. I believe the person we're looking for will be backstage somewhere. The center's security office said they had a replacement, but the security firm has backgrounds on everyone. They looked good," he remarked back through a smile. He wanted it to appear like the two of them were simply guests.

A moment later the mayor approached the two. "Hey, Johnny, who is your beautiful friend?"

The two shook hands warmly, then Watson introduced the mayor to Agent Trew of the FBI. "We actually have to work together tonight, Mr. Mayor. I sometimes draw the worst assignments."

"Watching Ringo Starr while next to a beautiful woman must be hell for you," the mayor said as he raised his glass. The lights in the foyer dimmed, alerting the crowd to move to their seats.

"You can take the main room. Watch for rifle barrels or hand guns. Although the metal detector should have eliminated them, our killer has his ways of making things happen when we think he can't," John instructed Trew. She nodded and sauntered through the door into the auditorium. He moved towards the back to the stage wings. He flashed his credentials at the man keeping people from getting too close to Ringo and the other All Stars. He walked behind the back scrim and made it to the other side of the stage. He looked up at the catwalk, but nothing could be seen. He radioed Trew. "I see nothing. How are things out there?"

"Clear," she answered.

Watson switched frequencies to listen in on the center's security checks. All seemed fine. Everyone was in their proper place. The band moved to the stage and took up their instruments. They played an intro for Ringo's big hit, "Photograph" and he ran onto the stage, pulled the microphone from the stand, and greeted everyone before launching into his big hit.

Then came an early Beatles number, "Boys." He introduced the band before telling the VIP audience that his next song would be "Yellow Submarine." That was one of the trigger songs John and Trew had decided would be a possibility.

Watson moved behind the stage, peering at every dark corner. Nothing. He raised his gaze to the catwalk above. A silhouetted figure moved slightly. That was all Watson needed to see. He scrambled for the twisting staircase that moved upward. He pulled his service revolver as he climbed silently. Once at the top, Watson peered over the edge. The silhouette was moving into a crouching position.

"Trew, he is on the catwalk," John said softly. Her response came back as a static garbling, John decided not to attempt another call for back-up from Trew. Instead he rose slowly until he was in a position to charge the figure. His movements, though low, slow, and quiet, were too much for the short space between them. The figure had already raised his rifle to his shoulder when he saw John. The shooter swiveled and aimed directly at John. At that range, all he could do was make himself a smaller target. He heard a pop but didn't hear or see a bullet go by him.

Watson raised his head. The figure was gone, and John heard steps on the spiral staircase at the other side of the stage. Watson leaped to his feet and ran for the other staircase. As he started to descend, he heard a door close at the bottom.

Because of the staircase design and Watson's athletic and bulky build, he couldn't get down to the bottom fast enough. When he did he opened the door to find a thin hallway leading to another door. That door came out on the hallway that surrounded the perimeter of the stage. Watson pushed open that door to find Trew on the other side with her gun drawn. She pointed it right at him as he raised his for the kill shot.

They both grimaced. She looked at him and said, "I couldn't understand what you said. My com was getting too much feedback. I decided to head backstage to see where you were."

"Did you see anyone come through here?"

"The hallway was empty when I got here. How did Bungalow Bill get away?" she asked with a frustrated tone.

"Go to the security office and check his tapes. I'm heading

to the catwalk. He left his weapon up there. Maybe there is something else I can find," Watson directed her.

***

She walked to the security office, flashed her credentials, and described where the incident took place. The guard gave her a sad look and shook his head from side to side before saying, "I wish I could help, but we don't have cameras on that side of the stage. It is one of our blind spots."

"Does every guard know it is a blind spot?" she asked.

"Even the new guy knew that," he answered.

"New guy?"

"Yeah, one of our guys called off sick and the firm sent over a new guy to replace him," the guard answered.

Trew was upset that she hadn't been informed. "Get your supervisor on the phone now."

He turned and dialed, then handed it to Trew. "Sir, this is Agent Trew of the FBI. Why weren't we informed that you had a change of personnel at the iWireless Center?" she snapped out with a terse and irritated voice.

The supervisor stammered on the other end of the line. "I am checking my records, but I don't see any replacement on the list."

She slammed the phone down. Turning to the guard in front of her, Trew said, "Who told you that there was replacement?"

"The guy walked in with all the correct paperwork, so I assumed it was legit. I also got a call from someone saying they were from the main office, and they gave me the sick personnel story. I am sorry, I just didn't know that I needed to contact you. The supervisor would have done that, and I assumed he had," the man said.

***

Trew exited and ran directly into John Watson. He was holding the shooter's rifle. She looked at it strangely. "It's a frigging toy rifle!" she blurted out.

"Yes, this whole night was a diversion," he said grimly. He knew if this had been a diversion then there was another killing on the horizon.

"What do we do now?" Trew asked as she leaned her body against the wall and blew out a long breath.

"I want all their surveillance tapes from tonight, and then we wait until he attacks again. I don't think it will be that long from tonight. In the meantime, we watch the concert," Watson said before entering into the camera room and asking for the surveillance videos and stowing his piece of evidence.

Watson walked out of the room, lifted Trew's hand from her side, and placed it under and over his arm. "Would you be my date for this fine affair?" he asked. Trew smiled and they headed down the hallway together. Moondog moved his face close to her neck and drew in a breath. "I really love that perfume."

"I am glad you do, but I was kind of hoping you would like me for me, and not just because I smell nice," Trew responded.

He smiled.

CHAPTER 31

The sun was just breaking through the clouds and the early morning mist. Over his shoulder he carried the lifeless form of a petite woman. He tiptoed through the strawberry plants as they were awakening to a sunny day. He trod lightly on the path that led between the maturing plants. Lush strawberries were already hanging low on each plant.

"I am so sorry, honey, but we have no time to stop and taste the luscious strawberries right now. Be patient, for once I put you down then we can have a berry apiece. Okay, maybe I will have two, if you don't mind." He stopped talking and kept up his walk to the center of the patch. "Here is the perfect spot for us to rest."

He lifted the small woman from his shoulder and placed her face up in the midst of several strawberry plants. "Be careful, dear, you are wearing a beautiful white dress. Did I tell you how nice you look in all that lace? Almost indescribable." The mad man placed her two hands together on her abdomen, then folded them in a prayerful gesture. He smiled then placed a musical greeting card underneath the hands. He had already recorded his message for Moondoggie.

"All this white in the middle of gorgeous red strawberries and their deep green leaves. Poetic," he whispered to the morning dew. He stood staring at his piece of art. With a finger to his chin, he noticed that her feet were not straight. "You need to look nice and proper as you head down the aisle,

159

my little lovely." The sun had risen further in the sky, and the light was dancing off the dew that hung from the berries and leaves. "The way the sun is carving through the dew-covered leaves and berries is absolutely lovely. Yes, what was that?" He cupped his hand to his ear. "Oh, yes, my dear. You are lovely, too. What a glorious day for your first communion. Your communion dress does look wonderful on you. Your purity is framed by nature's most delicious berries." He leaned in again and cupped his ear to hear her words. "Oh, yes, yes, yes. You are a wonderful model for this new masterpiece. I am so glad that I snatched you from the street."

He looked around and around like a man confused, then he saw what he wanted. "I did promise you a strawberry, didn't I?" He saw the largest, ripest one close to her head and plucked it. He pried open her lips and smashed it gently on her teeth until the red juices eked out of the berry and ran down the two sides of her mouth. He stood back and admired his work. Something was missing, he thought. Something needed to be added. Then it struck him. He searched for two smaller ripe and juicy berries. The first he pressed into her left eye until it ran down the side of her face towards her blonde hair and temple. He did the same with another on the other eye.

Satisfied, he stood back and stared. She was perfect. She may be his masterpiece, although he did still like Eleanor Rigby. His touch with the jar by the door was pure genius, he thought. He took a few steps back and, pulling out his camera, shot several shots from various angles. These were for his press kit. He had decided to definitely send these to the newspaper. It was time to ramp up the cat and mouse game.

After checking for any evidence he might have left, he tiptoed back through the strawberry plants. As he reached the edge he turned and blew the woman a kiss. Bungalow Bill raised his arms into the air and sucked in a large breath of the early morning air. Now it was time for the viewers to discover her.

CHAPTER 32

John "Moondog" Watson got into the office early to write up his report on the concert detail, and then go over the center's surveillance materials. Around 9 a.m. he had stood to get a cup of coffee from the machine when the captain banged open his door. "Watson, we got another one." Moondog felt ill, but at the same time had been expecting it.

"Tell me," Watson said.

"Out at Owen's Berry Farm. They found a body in the middle of —"

"The strawberry fields," John said. He took the information and walked towards the door. Lopez was strolling in when Watson grabbed him and spun him around. "We've got another body, and you are nominated to accompany me. Moses is at the doctor's this morning, so it is time for a little one on one time between us. Let's go."

The two hit the road and John spoke little. When the two arrived the investigation team was already on the scene. The farm manager was begging everyone not to mash the berries, but few listened to him. Watson and Lopez also tried unsuccessfully. They made it to the body. She had not been moved, and the greeting card was still tucked under her hands. Lopez talked to the officers to see who had discovered the body. The officer pointed to an attractive older woman and her grown daughter. He said their names were Sandy and Noni.

Lopez tiptoed over to them. "When did you discover the body?"

Sandy could barely speak, but said, "Around 8:30. We know the sun hits these strawberries the earliest, so they are the ripest."

"Did you notice anyone else here?" Lopez asked.

"No, it was just us, and Mr. Owen's truck was out in the blueberry fields. We guessed he was there. I noticed a white shape in the strawberries, but we couldn't see what it was until we were nearly on top of it," Noni answered.

"I'm going to have an officer escort you back to a squad car and get your contact information," he said as he touched both of them on their shoulders to give some comfort. Then he walked up to the body as he looked at his notebook. He stopped at the dead woman's feet and looked up. He suddenly felt sick. Very sick. His head spun, and he grabbed onto one his fellow policemen. His knees buckled.

Watson looked over at him. "Lopez, do you know the victim?"

Lopez pulled in a breath. "No, but I know the dress. My daughter has the same one. We bought it last week for her first communion. Before I saw the woman's face, I could only see the dress. My thoughts were racing, you know. I thought I was looking at my baby girl." Lopez pulled in a few more deep breaths, then straightened up.

"Are you going to be all right?" Watson asked.

"Yeah, only now I want this bastard as bad as anybody," Lopez said as he wiped sweat from his forehead. Lopez moved in closer. His eyes stared hard at the white face. He reached up and touched Moondog's shoulder, then said, "I recognize the woman. She was the one who sold us the dress."

"She worked at the department store?" John asked.

163

"Yes," Lopez answered.

"How did she die?" John asked.

"It looks like she was hung by the neck," the coroner answered. A line from the song ran through Moondog's head. *Nothing to get hung about.*

"Get me the card," Watson directed.

Using forceps, the coroner pulled the greeting card from under her hands and handed it to John, who opened it with gloved hands. He knew it was one with recorded message by the bulk inside the envelope. He also knew what song he would hear when he opened it up. He wasn't disappointed. "Strawberry Fields" played from the tiny replay speaker. The caption said, "Wish you were here instead of her."

Watson's phone rang. It was Moses. "John, I am guessing that you're at a strawberry field somewhere. I opened the morning paper and the lead story has a photo of a dead body in white with strawberry plants all around it. The headline reads, NOT A TERRORIST, BUT A SERIAL KILLER. This is not good news that he is sending out his own press releases with frigging photos with them."

"Meet me at the office and bring me the paper. I am heading there now," Watson said as he hung up his phone. "Let's go, Lopez. This Monday is getting worse by the minute." Watson filled in the new detective as they drove back. At the end of his telling what Moses had said, he looked directly at the young man and asked, "Where did you buy your daughter's communion dress?"

"Dillards at the North Park Mall. Do you want me to talk to people there to see who bought it?" Lopez asked.

"No. I need to pick up a few things today, so I will do it myself. I want you and Moses to get to the newspaper and see who the genius is who printed those photos. I want you to scare the life out of that man or woman."

John Watson sat at his desk and shuffled through the messages lying there. A Jody Johnson from the Figge Art Museum had called him and left messages three times that morning. Her messages said it was urgent. He crumbled them up and tossed them in the basket at his feet just before Moses walked in with a copy of the newspaper in his hands. He handed it to his mentor and sat in the seat across from him.

"This Bungalow Bill has got to be bat shit crazy. Why does he send out photos of his murders? Why does he dress them up? Why does he pose them?"

Moondog leaned back. "If I had those answers then we would have this guy in custody by now. He's not a normal killer or a normal serial killer. He's not driven by sex to do it. It is more than just revenge against me. I need to know what drives him," Watson said as he dropped the paper on his desk. He looked up at Moses. "I have a job for you and Lopez. He has the assignment, so go see him."

Moses stood and turned to John. "Thanks for asking about my doctor's appointment."

Watson just scoffed at him and motioned him away. Moses laughed and moved towards Lopez. John picked up the newspaper again as his phone rang.

Chapter 33

"Detective Watson," he said into the receiver.

"Detective, this is Jody Johnson at the Figge Art Museum. I saw the pictures in the newspaper, and I think you are approaching this whole case incorrectly."

Watson had already had a bad morning, and he wasn't about to let some artsy-fartsy jerk tell him what he was doing wrong.

He was ready to light into her when she said, "I know exactly what these pictures represent, and I have information that can play this maniac right into your hands."

"When can we meet?" John asked.

"When are you available?" she asked.

"See you in twenty minutes," he said as he dropped the phone into the cradle. He sighed. He was finally ready to take anybody's advice.

He rose, straightened his tie, and walked to his car. Twenty minutes later he parked on the street outside of the Figge. With instructions from several different museum employees he found her office, sighed, and knocked on the door. This Johnson woman better have something new and insightful, or he would arrest her for wasting his time.

An attractive woman in her fifties with stylish salt and pepper hair opened the door. She smiled, and it was a glowing grin. He looked her up and down and appreciated her form. He liked her already. He thought, she could lecture him on art

166

anytime. "I'm Detective Watson, and you must be Dr. Jody Johnson."

"Yes, I am. It is very nice to meet you, Detective, but please call me Jody." She directed him to a chair opposite her desk. "I apologize for being so pushy on the phone, but when I saw those pictures alongside the ones of the Asian woman and Eleanor Rigby, I thought I could help you."

Watson sat down and said, "Call me John." He pulled out a pad and his pen. "I am truly hoping you can help me. You said that you think I am approaching this all wrong. How so?"

"First of all, my background is in art history. I spend my time looking at old art trends and new art trends. You surely remember that John met Yoko at one of her art shows."

John fidgeted before saying, "Yes, but I don't really understand what that has to do with these killings."

"A lot more than you think. She was a conceptual artist that did installation pieces back towards the beginning of this whole phase of conceptual art. Do you know much about conceptual art?"

"Not a bit." He was completely honest. His art for his walls had come from big box stores designed to match his furniture.

"Many years ago, an artist named Marcel Duchamp made a point that art is the concept in the artist's head. He hung a urinal on the wall, signed it R. Mutt, and deemed it art. Therefore it was art. Out of that one act came the belief that art was the concept in the artist's head. If they called it art, then it was art."

"I guess art is in the eye of the beholder," John said as he loosened up his tie.

"Art is in the mind of the artist and the eye of the beholder.

That is the idea behind it. Conceptual artists began to do installation pieces. That is, they installed objects and called it art. It was Yoko's installation piece at the gallery that caught John's heart. Do you remember that one?" Jody asked as she hit keys on her computer and turned it around for Watson to see. "She placed a ladder in the room and above it, in small enough print that you had to climb the ladder to read it, she wrote the word 'Yes.' Lennon was so taken by the positive message that the two eventually got together, and the rest was Beatles history."

"Okay, so what does this have to do with my serial killer?" Watson said as he sighed. So far, his visit had been a waste of time in his opinion.

"Did you find a ladder at any of your crime scenes?" she asked.

He paused and thought, then it struck him. Sitting in the corner of the Davids' cottage there had been a ladder, but it didn't seem to have anything to do with the crime. "We did at the second crime scene."

"Did anyone climb it and look at the ceiling?" she asked with her dazzling and knowing smile.

"I think we were all trying to save the man's life. I did not stay for the crime scene investigation. The victim's life was ebbing away fast."

"Can you describe the scene?" she asked. "Give me as much detail as possible, and tell me how you felt and the thoughts you had."

Watson went into the details of the emaciated man and the dozens of donuts carefully placed around the starving body.

"Where are the donuts, and what kind are they?" she asked with a surprised voice.

"The donuts are in a freezer at the police station. They're just donuts. We still haven't found the bakery where they were bought."

"You need to check each one. There will be meaning to the kinds of donuts he placed there," she said, then moved back to her computer. She looked back at him and said, "You should send an officer to the cottage to see what is at the top of that ladder. It will be a clue, and most likely an important one." She motioned for Watson to go ahead and call the station to send an officer.

Watson called the station and had an officer check out the woman's theory. When he hung up she continued.

"Here is where I think you're being misdirected. You are a policeman looking at the crimes as a statement about the killer, or about something else—"

Watson interrupted her. "There is a strong vein of revenge towards me running through them. I just can't figure out who hates me this much."

"That is an interesting bit of information, and I need to factor that in. Can you describe another crime scene for me?" Jody asked as she leaned forward on her desk. The light caught her hair, and Watson's was distracted for a moment. He then talked about Eleanor that was killed in the church.

"And another?"

Watson went over the details of the judge's murder and the four others. She sat back and pressed her fingertips together, pursing her lips.

"Why don't you just figure out which song or songs are next and set a trap?" she queried.

"There are too many songs to cover every one of them. We are examining different scenarios, but there are still way too many to get ahead of the maniac," he answered tersely.

He was getting irritated once again with people telling him how to do his job.

"It is much simpler than you think," she told Watson while tipping her chair forward. "You are approaching the crime scenes like crime scenes designed to send you a message. You're wrong. They're not trying to send you a message. They are the message. Look at it from an art historian's point of view."

Watson let out a deep sigh. This woman may be as crazy as the man he was trying to catch. He shut his notebook and slipped it into his pocket. He needed to cut the discussion short before he lost any more valuable time.

She noticed his frustration and folded her hands. She looked straight at him and said, "I can tell you what his next couple of song choices are. If you are so god-awful sure of your methods, then you won't catch him until he is done building his body of art work. These are all pre-conceived art pieces designed to make one complete statement."

Watson dropped back into his seat. "Give me something good so I can catch him."

"From the art historian's point of view, the killer is a conceptual artist choosing to do installation piece art work based on images inside Beatles songs. The songs have to elicit a certain kind of image in his head. That is his concept. Once he builds the concept in his mind, then the artist must assemble all the pieces and put them together. Only a few songs have that potential."

He opened his notebook again and listened.

She spoke again. "There is one more thing you need to know." Watson sat forward to make sure he caught every word. "There was one other artist that used dead animals to build an installation piece close to twenty or twenty-five years ago in Boston. I can't remember the time frame. He entitled his show, *The Stench of Death.*"

"Nice, positive, up title," Watson joked.

"Yeah, I know. The gallery thought he was installing sculptures of dead animals, like a roadkill museum. No, he used real dead animals. By the third day of the show, the stench was horrendous and maggots were creeping from carcasses. He and his 'art works' were tossed out of the gallery. That's all I can remember reading. I've searched the Internet, but no additional information came up."

"Do you remember the name of the artist who created *The Stench of Death* art show?"

"I don't remember reading his name," she answered while shaking her head from side to side.

Watson remarked, "You have really helped me, and I need to check out this information. I need to run, but could you call me later with the list of songs you believe the killer will use?" Watson rose from the chair slowly, and then walked out of her office. If she was right, he needed to look at every murder in a different light.

CHAPTER 34

Watson had barely turned into the police station when a call came in on his cell. It was the officer that had been sent to the David's cottage. "Detective, I climbed the ladder like you said. There are no words written on the ceiling, but there is a glob of something."

"Describe it," Watson snapped.

"Just a reddish, dried blob."

"Scrape it into an evidence bag and take it to the lab for analysis. First though, take a picture — then, after you get if off, take another picture. There should be something underneath," John responded, then hung up. He spoke to himself as he walked up the steps to the station. "So, you arrogant bastard, you gave me a hidden clue. I won't miss it the next time."

As John Watson stepped into the police station, he motioned with his head for Moses to follow him into the conference room. Watson stood with his hands on his hips and his coat pushed back away from them. He was staring hard. Without asking, Sammy closed the door. He knew the pensive look that crossed his partner's face. He had something that he was holding close to his chest, and now he was about to unveil it. Moses waited patiently, picking at imaginary lint on his coat. He knew not to hurry it.

Moondog spun around and walked quickly to a metal chair that sat before their crime board. He dropped to the chair and sighed. Moses grabbed another and sat it next to

172

Watson. "I went to see an art professor at the Figge today," Moondog said, then he smiled. "I was irritated at first because she said we were approaching the killings like murders."

Moses scrunched up his face, as if to say "How else do you approach it?" John held up his hand to keep the questions from coming.

"I know what you want to say, and that is exactly how I reacted to her criticism; then she proved it to me. She said that each murder was laid out like what she called a conceptual art installation piece. Then she told me how John and Yoko met at one of Yoko's gallery installation pieces." John held up a hand to keep Moses quiet. "She said that John was so impressed with one of her pieces that she captured his heart. The piece had to do with a ladder and a single word written at the top of it." Moondog turned to Moses and looked him square in the eye before saying, "Do you remember a ladder at any of the crime scenes?"

Sammy sat for a moment. "Yeah, I leaned against one at the David cottage. I thought it was out of place, but not out of the ordinary."

"Exactly. Well, I sent a black and white to the cottage. He found the ladder and climbed it. He found a reddish glob on the ceiling. He's bringing it back here for analysis, but he is also taking a picture of anything that might be under the glob. We'll know in a few minutes about his findings.

"But she told me something else that I found strangely connected." Watson stood up and wrote the word Boston on the white board. "In Boston, which was the city that Officer Marylee McCarren had written down on her undiscovered note, there was an art show by one of those conceptual installation artists where the guy, calling himself an artist, brought in a bunch of dead animals and made his art piece out of carcasses." John wrote the words *dead animals* on the board.

John picked up an office phone extension from the table near him and called the lab. "Pagley, this is Watson. What kind of donuts did we find at the David cottage?" He waited for the lab tech to grab the report. After Pagley told him what they were, John went back to the board. He wrote *jelly* on it, and the words *Boston cream*.

"Shit, we've been missing clues. That art woman is really onto something. What else did she say?" Moses asked.

"Each killing is like another painting being hung in his gallery of sick art work. We keep looking for fingerprints and hairs and DNA, and this guy is leaving us all the pertinent clues we need." He looked at Moses without saying a word. Then after drawing in a long deep breath, Watson exhaled.

"She said that only certain songs have the potential to fulfill his murder visuals. I think she is right. She is going to give me a list, and we are going to post cops at every possibility." He clapped his hands together. "We're going to get out ahead of him, and he will walk into our trap."

John Watson had taken two steps towards the door when the officer who had gone to the Davids' cottage appeared. He held up his phone and showed the detective a picture of the ceiling. On the ceiling was written the word YES. It was the same thing Yoko had written at the top of the ladder. The word that had made John Lennon seek her.

The officer held out the bag with the scraped blob. Watson took one look at it and handed it back. He already knew what it was — strawberry jelly. John reeled around towards Moses and spoke, "Wipe everything off the board. From now on, only you and I will know the exact nature of what is going on." Then he spun towards the door and left.

CHAPTER 35

Watson's next stop was his brother Matt's house. Matt had the door open before John reached the top of the twenty steps. "Something new has come up, I take it."

Watson smiled at his baby brother and spoke while walking through the door. "I need a search for an old art exhibit. It was twenty to twenty-five years ago. It happened in Boston."

"Nothing like giving me an impossible job to do. Good thing that Mel is at work." The two walked into Matt's office and huddled behind the computer. "Do you have any more clues than that?"

"The show was called *The Stench of Death*. The artist dumped dead animals into the gallery and let them rot. I imagine we'll find something in the Boston newspapers from that period. I want the artist's name, the gallery name, and the gallery owner's name." He stopped, then looked at Matt. "If anyone can find something out it will be you. So, snap to it." John stood up and asked, "Do you have any cold beer? I can use one about now."

"Fridge, bottom shelf. Get me one, too," Matt answered as his fingers flew across the keyboard. By the time John walked back in the room, Matt was printing out the first article he'd found. "It was twenty-three years ago. The gallery was called Avant Garage. The place had to close down after that because the stench left by the rotting animals wouldn't go away. The owner, a Jeffrey Hoyt, went bankrupt after that. The artist was a Randy Scanland."

"Nothing there rings a bell. Do a search on Hoyt. Try to find me some contact information. See what kind of financial records are out there on him," John requested.

"It looks like he died in the late nineties. Actually, it says he was killed in a boating accident. Not much else on him." Matt sat back. "Want to try Randy Scanland?"

"Sure," John said as he tipped his beer can back and drained the last of the liquid. He left the office to grab another beer. As he walked back in the door, he found Matt with a puzzled look on his face. "What did you find?"

"I've had some trouble finding anything on an artist named Scanland, but here is a fact I am surprised you didn't know," Matt said as he looked over his shoulder at his big brother. "Randolph Peter Scanland was the birth name of none other than former Beatle, Pete Best."

John put his can down on the desk and pushed Matt away from the screen. He read, then scrolled down and read some more. It finally made sense. Watson grabbed the print-out from the website and headed to the door, yelling over his shoulder, "I know who you are, you sick bastard." As he pulled the front door open he yelled back to his brother, "Thanks. I think you just broke this case wide open."

His first call once in the car was to Jody Johnson. She wasn't in. He left a message for her to call him right away. With the new information, she should be able to pinpoint the right songs. He hung up and was ready to dial Moses when Moses called him.

"There's a package at the station for you. No return address. I had it printed already," Moses reported.

"Send it down to the bomb squad to open. I think

Bungalow Bill is getting desperate. I want it ready for me to see when I get there." Moondog hit the end button on his phone. He hoped this would be the last killing before he could stop the maniac.

A few minutes later, Watson pulled into the station and walked inside. Moses was holding a CD up in the air for him to see. "I thought I'd let you do the honors, boss." The younger detective lifted a boom box from off the filing cabinets and laid it on Moondog's desk, then dropped the CD into the player. Watson took a breath and pushed the play button.

He knew the song from the first note. "Lady Madonna" was impossible to mistake, with the Fats Domino influences and the hard rhythm. John ran through his life, trying to come up with a scenario that merged his history, Beatle history, and an insane artist's take on how to present the song.

"Isn't this one about a nun or the Virgin Mary?" Moses asked as Watson pushed the off button when the song ended.

Watson turned away and stared out of the window. Images were moving like puffy clouds across a blue sky. They were wispy, then started to form. He rotated back to Moses and said, "It started out that way, but ended up being more about a hard-working single mother." He paused. His silence made Moses nervous, but the cop knew better than to interrupt at that point. Moondog pulled in a long breath. "Bungalow Bill will go for the stronger visual, so he will use a nun, but he won't miss the alternate meaning. For sure, he has it tied to something in my past." He paused again while he paced the room in deep thought.

"The Moondogs played three different churches, for their teens, back in the beginning—St. Marys, which he already used; St. Marks, which I barely remember; and St. Johns was in a garden that sat surrounded by the buildings. It was mostly girls at that venue. They screamed like we were the real Beatles. I remember us all getting into trouble with this old nun for flirting with the girls. She was a mean old bag, at least we thought so." Watson stopped. He smiled. "One of us got caught making out with this girl in the bushes right behind the nun. She took a ruler to him. I think Jelly had blisters for a week." Watson smiled at the memory, then focused again on the song. "Our dead nun is at St. Johns in the garden. Call the investigation team to meet us there."

As Moses made the calls to the crime investigation team, Moondog picked up the extension on his desk and dialed Jody Johnson. Her phone rang a few times, then went to voicemail. She was obviously tied up. That fact bothered him. Bungalow Bill had gotten to witnesses before he could stop him. He tried to remember if anyone besides Moses knew about her. He pulled his wastebasket close and looked inside for the phone messages he had gotten earlier to give her a call. He rummaged through the basket, but no messages were there. He searched a second time, but still there was nothing.

Watson lifted the phone and called the Figge Museum. "Is Dr. Johnson in?"

"She stepped out. We expect her back any minute now. Can I tell her who called?"

"Yes, tell her to call Detective Watson immediately. This is urgent," he responded.

CHAPTER 36

As Moondog stepped out of the car, he was impacted by images of his youth. He looked at the garden through the gate that hung between the high limestone walls. They had added a maintenance building where the cement patio had been, creating a smaller garden. Even the smaller garden looked unused. The grass was high, almost obscuring the stepping stones that moved from one pastoral seating area to another. He flashed back to the day the Moondogs had played. He felt the youth and vibrancy. He felt the hormones of a big group of teens dancing to their music.

Johnny and the Moondogs weren't the best band then. They were still young, and they were still raw in their abilities. He could almost see the girls dressed in their long dresses, with headbands filled with baby's breath flowers, peace symbol necklaces dangling on their chests. The few boys were letting their hair grow out over their collars.

The Moondogs' music pounded off the stone walls in the garden. He felt himself swaying to the sounds in his head. Somewhere inside him, Watson longed for those simpler days of rock 'n' roll. Instead, when he heard the songs of his youth, he panicked that there was another murder, another twisted, deadly picture of death.

"John, are you all right?" Moses asked, but John "Moondog" Watson was still stuck in memories. John shifted his head towards his partner, nodded once, and then smiled.

179

He had a recollection of a large nun with glaring eyes. She was shaking a ruler and screaming at John.

"Keep your heathen band members away from the girls. I thought you were good Catholic boys," she bellowed. He could remember trying his best not to laugh. His band was doing exactly what boys did. They were flirting with the girls. Nothing heinous, just flirting. Just being boys at a dance.

The real problems didn't come until after the second set of songs. John and Jimmy were getting something to drink when they heard a scream from the other side of the garden. There was a small alcove with an arch of roses at the opening. First came the scream, then came the large nun pulling Jelly Johnson by the ear, twisting it hard. His face winced with pain. A young girl with her lipstick smeared followed behind them. Her faced burned red with embarrassment.

The nun pulled Jelly over to the group leader, Johnny, giving his ear one last hard twist, and pushed him at Moondog. She was intensely furious. As she spoke, spittle flew from her mouth. "This young man was violating one of our girls. I will deal with her. He is banned from the church property forever. May his soul rot in Hell for this. He is the devil incarnate, and he will come to no good in this world." Watson shook his head at the prophetic memory.

Watson's memories ended. He sucked in a breath and turned to Moses. "Did you find her?"

"I don't see any sign of a murder here. Are you sure this is the right place?" Moses questioned.

"Right church, but we're in the wrong pew. Come with me." John strolled over to the where the old alcove with the rose arch had stood. The vining roses were unkempt. Their fragrant red flowers were drooping down from the top of the rotting archway. Moondog brushed them back with new

180

pruning shears he found leaning against the wall. He shivered. New pruning shears meant something bad had happened. As he pushed the roses to the side he could see the large wooden cross designed to aid in meditation, but it wasn't empty.

Moses peeked in behind him, then spun and wretched on the ground nearby. The scene was gruesome. An elderly nun had been nailed to the cross. She had died with her eyes frozen in traumatic fear. Watson moved closer. Her lips had been stapled shut, and blood covered one side of her white wimple head covering. Watson pulled a pen from his pocket and moved the covering away. He knew he would find a missing ear. The last image he saw were the tips of the fingers sheared off by the new shears he had found. The blood that had run from her fingertips to the wooden cross told John that these were done before the crucifixion. The killer made this murder more personal because it was personal. Without a doubt, John knew exactly who the killer was. All he needed to do was get ahead of him and this nightmare would be over.

Dr. Jody Johnson flashed into his mind. She understood where he might strike again. She was his key to capturing Bungalow Bill. Unfortunately, she was missing. That wasn't a good thing in Watson's mind. He pulled out his phone and dialed her number. It rang, then went to voice mail.

As the crime investigation team came in through the garden gate, Detective Watson told Moses he needed to check something out, and that he should head up the investigation. Watson hurried out of the gate to the car. He tried to call Johnson two more times before arriving at the Figge Museum. He parked in front with his lights flashing, and ran into the museum's main lobby. He flashed his badge, then raced to Dr. Johnson's office. He was hoping he would find her sitting at her desk. She wasn't.

He dialed her cell again. He heard it ring at his feet. Watson looked down, then realized it was under her desk, along with a hand written list of five songs. She had started the list and then was taken, or simply disappeared. He looked around for signs of a struggle, but there were none. He next moved to the hallway, where he saw two security guards moving quickly his way. Their hands were on their guns.

The taller one asked, "Is there a problem, sir?"

Watson flashed his badge. "I am trying to get hold of Dr. Johnson. Did anyone see anything suspicious in the museum or near her office? Did she leave with someone?"

The second guard spoke. "She said nothing to anyone when she left. She simply hurried to her car and drove away. I was watching her. She seemed distressed when she passed me by. I asked her if everything was all right, but she acted as if she never heard me."

"She was alone then?"

"Yes, Detective, she was alone, but seemed distressed," the guard answered.

John stepped back into her office and grabbed the handwritten note, then exited her office and the museum quickly. Before reaching his car, his phone vibrated in the chest pocket of his sports coat. He was afraid to look. A dreadful vision of Jody Johnson dead at the hands of Bungalow Bill was running through Watson's brain, but he had to answer.

He pushed the button and music floated out of the phone's speaker. It was a Beatles song, but not one he would have thought. It was "You Know My Name." Bungalow Bill's true identity was now known to Moondog. He knew the one person it had to be. His last few clues were too clear and pointing in only one direction. He did know the killer's name, but it was the second line of the lyrics that fogged his

182

reasoning. "Look up the number." Watson glanced at his phone. His caller ID showed a number. Did Bungalow Bill want to talk? Did he want Watson to listen to the cries of Jody Johnson as he killed her? What did he want? There was only one way for Moondog to find out.

CHAPTER 37

Watson sat on a marble bench in the sculpture garden at the Figge Museum and ended the call. He pushed a few buttons and called back the number on his caller ID.

"Hey, Johnny, long time, no talk."

The voice was unmistakably his old friend. It had seasoned over the years. It was more mellow and a bit deeper, but still the voice he remembered from over forty years before. It was steady but menacing, and at the same time still tinged with boyish friendship. "I'm glad you called back. Just like the song says, you know who I am, and now, Moonie, you know my number."

Moondog Watson calmed himself before he spoke. He didn't want to sound scared or antagonistic. "Hello, Jelly."

"I thought you would call me Bungalow Bill. I'm just tinkled pink that you remember my voice. We haven't talked since the night you threw me out of the band." Jelly's voice was still calm, but a little less friendly.

"Jelly, you didn't play well enough and you kept missing practices. What was I to do?" John talked slowly, keeping accusations and anger out of his tone. He waited for Jelly Jefferson to speak again. It was a long pause.

"I bet you wish you hadn't done that, now. Payback is a bitch, Johnny," Jelly said. His smirk was evident in his voice. There was another pause.

"How is killing innocent people a payback to me, Jelly?

Your acts of revenge have put many families in agony. Your selfishness has ruined lives," Moondog answered in a calm voice. "So, what do you want from me?"

"I am getting what I want. I am ruining your career. I am hurting you badly," he said.

"Tell me, how did you know I figured out who you were?" Moondog asked.

"I guess it wouldn't hurt to tell you. Throughout my life, I have been planning this. I have set trip wires in my digital trail. When someone searches for certain items, I'm alerted. That all comes along with being a computer genius. By the way, how is little Matty? I always liked that kid when you brought him to the practices. Too bad you involved him in this—" Jelly said before he was interrupted.

"You sick bastard. If you hurt him, then I will find a way to punish you like you've never been punished before." Watson's voice exploded as he said it.

"Calm down, Johnny, calm down. Matty was my little buddy, too. I've put a virus in his computer system. He'll lose all his equipment, but I'm not going to hurt the kid."

John physically calmed down and tempered his voice. "Why are you doing this, Jelly?"

"The perfect answer would be: because I can. Which is true, but not the real answer. I'm destroying you, and that gives me great pleasure. After Sexy Sadie died in childbirth, I remembered how you treated her. I remembered the bad things you said about her, and—"

John interrupted again. "I never said a word about her. It was students in school that trashed her. I never did."

"Not the way I remember it. And really, how I remember things is the only thing that matters."

Watson waited a minute before speaking again. "So,

where is she?"

"Who? Oh, you mean Prudence. She is most likely at the police station looking for her lover boy cop. How in the world did you land a nice girl like that? Or maybe she is as obsessed as you are with this Bungalow Bill character that you created," Jelly responded, but his response told Moondog one thing. He did not know about Jody Johnson.

"Turn yourself in, Jelly. We can get you the mental help you need," said John.

"What, and stop my fun? End my revenge?" Jelly paused for a moment before saying, "I have a better idea. Why don't you just catch me? Why don't you try to outsmart me? You can't do it, huh, Johnny? You were never smarter than me. I'm a genius, you know. That's what they said at MIT before I was thrown out. I'm a genius, Johnny, and you're a fat Quad Cities cop."

"You are insane. Do you know that, Mr. Genius?" Watson spat out.

"Sticks and stones, Johnny, sticks and stones." The call ended.

A moment later his phone rang again. It was the hospital.

"Detective Watson, this is Jody. I hope I'm not disturbing anything," she said.

"I was worried sick. I called all afternoon, then went to your office. I found your phone and thought the worst," he replied with both relief and chastisement in his voice.

"Sorry, I got a call that my mother was rushed to the hospital. I ran out so fast that I dumped my purse. My phone must have fallen under my desk." There was a pause. John heard her talking to a nurse, then she came back on the line. "I am almost done here. They admitted my mother. Once I get her settled in a room, we can meet to discuss the list that I am sure you found as well," the art professor said.

"Call me when you are ready," he said, then added, "I will go back into your office and grab your phone."

"Thanks. I should be done in about an hour," she said, then hung-up.

CHAPTER 38

John "Moondog" Watson had some private thinking to do before going over Jody's list with her. Abbey Road, his Beatles memorabilia shop, was open, and his salesperson was surprised to see him when he walked through the door. Sabrina was showing a customer a few of the earlier Beatles albums when she looked up at him through her large black glasses. She was a pretty girl, with a quick wit and a wry sense of humor. She was also the daughter of an old family friend. She knew her counter culture, which made her the perfect person to run the store.

"Do you have any suggestions for someone just starting to listen to the Beatles?" She motioned with her head towards a tall, thin kid with a scruffy beard, two piercings in his nose, and several earrings hanging from his ears. Moonie smiled. His favorite band was still attracting listeners from across the generations.

Moonie looked at the boy and said, "Do you want straight up rock 'n' roll, or a bit of experimental mixed in?"

"Rock 'n' roll. I like it stripped down and rocking," he answered, with lots of emphasis on the word rocking.

"Their second album was always my favorite," Moonie answered, then headed for his office and shut the door. He had work to do, and Sabrina could easily handle the situation with more poise and concentration than he had left in his body.

Moonie pulled the folded list from Dr. Johnson from his pocket and dropped it on the desk. Then he reached into his breast pocket and removed the two folded lists that he and Agent Trew had made, along with Trew's compilation. He unfolded all four and smoothed them on the surface before him.

The detective pushed his hair back from his forehead as he stared at the many songs before him. He compared his original list to Jody's. All five of her songs were on his. He compared Trew's list, and three of Jody's songs were on hers. Then he reviewed the compilation Trew had made of his list and her list. There were no matches.

His mind raced as he left his office for the coffee pot in the back. Sabrina always had coffee on, and it was always good coffee. He poured a cup and looked over at the girl. She was selling three albums to the boy. Either the kid had a real interest in the Beatles or he had a real interest in Sabrina. He smiled and went back into his office, pulling the door closed behind him.

He needed to decide how to get out ahead of Bungalow Bill, aka Jelly Jefferson. It would be more like a game of chess. He had approached his list like a cop. He'd looked for clues that would help him win the battle. Trew had approached hers from what she could assume from the killer's profile. Jody's was based on the assumption that Bungalow Bill saw himself as a conceptual, installation artist.

His real problem was that he assumed there was either a mole or a bug, or both, at the police station. He had to misdirect, and he had to keep his real direction from the other officers. He knew he could trust Moses. Lopez had been on the force long enough that he assumed he was not the mole or the bug, but he decided to keep Moses only in his loop.

Everyone else, his suspicious mind would keep in a narrow loop.

He chose ten songs that he believed would be the most likely to be used next by Bungalow Bill. He would split the officers into ten groups, and they would surveil all ten locations. He went to his computer and made up ten packets that included the song title, the lyrics, and his selections for the possible locations. He put all ten in different envelopes and sealed them. Late that afternoon he would gather his team and make their assignments.

As he inserted the last pages into an envelope, his phone rang. Dr. Johnson was ready to meet him. He suggested the coffee shop that he and Moses had used earlier on in the investigation, because he felt it would be unwatched and not bugged. He put the envelopes in his side coat pocket, then headed for the front store door. He stopped for a minute to let Sabrina know he thought she did a good job.

"Wasn't that hard," she said, then widened her smile. "That kid was more into me than into the Beatles. Are you going to take any shifts in the next few days?"

"Can't. Call your friend Christie. See if she will help out."

"Will do, but that means you will be in, 'cause you think Christie is cute," Sabrina said to Moonie's back as he walked towards the door.

"You are cute too, but there is a big age spread, little girl," he shot back.

"The new FBI girlfriend is a lot younger than you. What is she, twenty years younger? She could be your daughter, or at least somebody's daughter," Sabrina said with sarcastic smile.

Moonie pretended to pull a knife from his back. "How bad do you need this job?" Moonie joked back as he cocked his head to the side.

"Not as bad as you need me, old man," she snapped back, almost laughing.

"Yeah, you've got a point there," as he pointed at her. He turned towards the door to leave, then turned back towards her. "Why do you think that Agent Trew is interested in me? Yeah, I am kinda cute, but I really am close to two decades older than her. I wonder about it."

"Maybe she just has bad taste in men. Maybe she's got daddy issues. Maybe she is trying to kill you with wild sex. Maybe she just likes you." Sabrina paused. "Maybe she just thinks you are a great guy." She placed her finger near her mouth as if she were pondering her last statement. "Nah!"

"Thanks for building me up," he said as he finally exited the door.

Moondog got to the coffee shop at the same time as Jody Johnson. He held the door open for her as he asked about her mother.

"She has a bad ticker. She scares me. I wish I could convince her to go into a facility where she had 24/7 care. Maybe this will give her a wake-up call." She paused, then said, "Probably not. She's hard headed, like her daughter."

As she spoke John guided her to a table at the back. He took the seat with a wall behind him. It was habit.

Johnson got right to the task at hand. "So, what do you think of my list?"

He reached into his pocket and extracted the four folded pieces of paper. One of them was her list. He flattened it and turned it around so she could read it. "Give me your reasons for each song."

"The first one is 'A Day in the Life.' How could he resist that line about blowing his mind out in a car, especially since it would involve some kind of political figure? That would be far too tempting. The visual could be very strong. It would be street art, and I don't think he could resist a forage into street art," she answered as the waitress brought two cups of coffee.

"I see that one. The mayor is a friend of mine, so there is a connection to me as well. It would be a definite slap to me and my career to have the mayor killed on my watch. Your next one was 'Paperback Writer.' I don't see that one," John questioned as he sat back in the booth seat.

"Thursday night there is a book reading at the Midwest Writing Center. They're having a *New York Times* bestselling author in to read from his latest big hit," Jody said as she trailed her finger along the song title. "It would be a dramatic scene no matter how he does it. People would be writing about it and Bungalow Bill for a long time after that." She sat back and said, "'Baby You're a Rich Man' would also be very high profile. A murder at one of the mansions would be a great background to one of his installation pieces."

"There are a lot people and homes that could fit that bill. How do we know who?" he asked.

"The rich man in the song kept all his money in a brown bag at the zoo. That means the rich man is either a big game hunter or he keeps exotic animals on the estate." She stopped, but her eyes were twinkling. "Charles Davenport is big game hunter. He has stuffed animals all over his ten-bedroom home. I've been there, and I've seen most of them." She then sat forward and smiled. "He is in town and throwing a gala this Saturday night. I have an invitation with a plus one. Interested?"

"You are beginning to amaze me. I would be honored to go along as your escort." Moonie shook his head and sat back with a gigantic smile on his face. "Now what about 'Get

Back'? I can see the images from the song lyrics, but have no idea as to what it could mean to the killer. We do have a drag club, but no ties into my background."

"You're talking about Connections, the club in town that does drag shows. If you remember, Sweet Loretta was a man who thought he was a woman. The other name in the song was JoJo. This Friday night is their next show, and their biggest name will be there — JoJo Lovelace. Bungalow Bill could do some dramatic things with that setting," she enlightened him. "Which brings us to my last song. 'Come Together' would be his final piece. His masterpiece, you might say. It is rife with strange images."

John opened another of the four notes in front of him and asked, "What about 'Happiness Is a Warm Gun'? That one seems to be perfect for the killer."

"Bang, bang, and it is over. No visual. No art. No installation piece. Too bland," she said as she dismissed it with her hand and a quick shake of her head.

"What about 'Don't Let Me Down,' or 'I Am the Walrus'? Both have some strange images."

"Detective, the songs I gave you are the ones that tie into local happenings. Even Eleanor Rigby had a church wedding that day." She drew in a breath. "He is using current events to build more lasting images. He is a mad man, yes, but he is also a genius. You need to think like him to catch him." She checked her watch. "I better get back to the hospital. Call me tonight and we can go over these more in depth. I will listen to these five songs again while I think like the killer slash artist. I should get some good visuals."

John Watson watched her rise from the table and head to the door. He hadn't noticed before, but she was an especially attractive woman even from behind. John threw a ten-dollar bill down to cover the coffees, rose, and walked to his car. He felt like he finally had a plan.

CHAPTER 39

Watson had called ahead to have Moses gather the officers who had been working on the Bungalow Bill case. As he pushed the doors open, Moses was standing by his desk gathering up folders of the information that had come in during the day. The head detective wasn't interested in those. All past research was designed to find the real identity of Bungalow Bill. Since his conversation with Jelly Jerry Jefferson, that line of inquiry was finished. He had one goal in mind. John Watson was now the hunter, and he could smell the prey like the drips of blood in the ocean for a shark.

"Officers, I now know who our killer is. Let me explain, so have a seat," he announced loudly.

The plainclothes and uniformed officers found seats. There was a hushed buzz of conversation about how Watson did it. Once everyone was seated, Watson removed his coat and loosened his tie. He had a smile on his face. Agent Trew looked seriously puzzled as she sat in the front seat. He grinned down at her. He was sure she wasn't expecting what he was about to say.

"This afternoon, after the 'Lady Madonna' killing, I had a feeling that I had solved the riddle of who Bungalow Bill really is. I was about to check out a few items to confirm my hunch when I received a phone call. The song was 'You Know My Name.' I looked at my caller ID and the number was not blocked. As the Beatles song invited, I gave the number a call. I recognized the voice quickly, and the two of us talked. Agent Trew had been right on the money with her assessment. The killer had a connection to me, and desired to ruin my reputation. Congratulations on that fine work, Agent Trew.

"As the killer and I talked, he explained to me that all this was revenge for me letting him go as the drummer of my band way back in high school. Our killer is Jerry Jefferson. He had a nickname of Jelly, since that was about all he would eat." Watson moved to his coat and pulled out the envelopes he had prepared that afternoon. "Obviously, the investigation into the who and why is over. It is time to try and get ahead of him. We want to prevent his next killing, capture him, and bring the lunatic to trial," the lead detective told his team. He climbed onto a high stool, sat down, and flashed the envelopes in front of the crew. "Inside these envelopes are ten different Beatles songs, their lyrics, and some insights from me. I am grouping you into teams of two. You will get an envelope, but you can't reveal it to any other team."

Several hands shot into the air. Questions flew at him quickly. He held his hands up to ask for silence. "Why am I doing that?" he asked before he smiled and gave the answer. "We have a mole, or we have a bug that we can't find in this room. This means that keeping your assignment to yourselves keeps the listening ears or the prying mole from knowing what songs I've chosen."

Moondog Watson grabbed the units that already worked as partners and handed them their envelopes. He put Jerry Lopez and Prudence Trew together. He walked them to the corner and whispered to them. "Once you look inside you will see why I put the two of you together. Trew, you will have to protect Lopez. Let me know how you decide to handle it. I may even be part of your team for this one." He walked away.

They couldn't see his smile.

The teams left for quiet settings far away from the police station. Once they were all gone, Watson and Moses left together, heading for their out of the way coffee shop. John had a lot to tell his partner, and only his partner. As they slid into seats, Watson pulled out the four folded pieces of paper and slid them to Moses.

"This list is the one I compiled with Trew. This one she compiled. This is our lists placed together. The final list was made by a PhD at the Figge. She rearranged my thinking on why Bungalow Bill was choosing the songs he did. I believe she has deciphered his reasons correctly," John said as he sat back. They both ordered coffee from the waitress. As she walked away, Watson started again. "Some of the teams have these five songs, including Trew and Lopez. They have 'Get Back.' We will be the back-up on all of them."

"What was this art woman's reasoning for these five?" Moses inquired.

"Good visuals and links to current events in the Quad Cities," he answered. Watson ran down the possible current events. John wrote the dates of each next to the song titles. "I believe the mayor is the target for 'A Day in the Life.' We need to draw the killer into a trap on that one, but he will need a day or two to plan." Moondog smiled. "And so do we."

"What about the others?" Moses asked.

"On Thursday night, we hit the Midwest Writing Center for their reading. Swing by the Rock Island library today and find out where they are going to do the reading. Then we can see how to set our trap there." Watson jotted more notes down on his note from Jody Johnson. "Friday we hit Connections with Trew and Lopez. The show doesn't start until eleven. We should have time to set a trap there." Watson wrote more notes down while the waitress filled their coffee cups.

Moses looked up at him. "Should I notify this JoJo?"

"No, no, no," Moondog said quickly. "Four cops there should be enough to deter a killing, but if this JoJo knew what was going on then things could unravel quickly, and we would never catch Bungalow Bill."

"It seems to me that you have a lot of the plans already conceived, and that you are confident in this art doctor's five songs," Moses said while pointing at the list in front of him. "And, I should add, you're ignoring Agent Trew's list."

John loosened his tie. He took another sip of coffee, then spoke. "I think Jody has the right take on this one." He paused for a moment. "One thing that made me think she was right was a failed art show called *The Stench of Death*. My gut tells me that was Jelly in an earlier part of his life. That one key convinced me that I needed to run with Dr. Johnson's insights."

"Then what about this 'Baby You're a Rich Man' song for Saturday night?" Moses questioned.

"Charles Davenport is throwing a gala at his place. The lyrics in the song point towards that man, that house, and that song. The doctor and I will attend the gala. It will be up to me to find and capture Jelly Jefferson." Watson folded his four pages and put them back in his pocket. Moses had a puzzled look on his face.

"What about the last one, 'Come Together'?"

"She thinks it will be his last one, and his masterpiece. To be honest, I have no clue as to where or what that one will be. Hopefully something comes in that gives me a little guidance. Or better yet, we capture him long before Bungalow Bill gets to that." John stood and dropped a few dollars on the table for the coffee. He passed Moses, who was still sitting.

Before he stood, Sam Moses asked one last question, "Do you think you'll catch him before that one?"

"Nope," John said over his shoulder. "It won't end until one of us is dead. I'm planning on it being him."

CHAPTER 40

Before heading home for an evening of greatly needed rest, John "Moondog" Watson put a call into Mayor Mark Edwards office to make an appointment. He stopped by a Casey's General Store for two large coffees — one black for him, and one with two sugars and extra cream for the mayor. The two had been friends since Edwards first ran for city council. Moondog's wife and the mayor's future wife had worked at a North Park Mall department store while finishing up their degrees. Jessica Watson had set up a blind date between Keesha, her friend from work, and John's friend, Councilman Edwards. The two hit it off immediately, and the rest was history, as the saying goes.

Watson walked into the mayor's office. Mark rose from behind his desk and motioned for the two of them to sit at the chairs around a low table near the center of the room. They shook hands and sat.

John leaned forward. "I've made contact with our killer."

The mayor leaned back in his chair and sighed. Edwards knew that wasn't the end of the story. "Tell me everything," he said.

John went over the high school history of Jerry "Jelly" Jefferson and what he knew of his years in between. Then he described the phone call and the meetings with Dr. Jody Johnson. As Watson finished and sat back in his chair, the mayor spoke again.

"I am betting that this visit isn't an FYI get together. There is more to all this."

"As I mentioned, the art professor gave me five songs that she believes he will use to finish out his killing spree. I believe those are all very viable possibilities. I believe his next attempt will be the song, 'A Day in the Life,'" Watson said.

"I don't really know the lyrics to that one. How does it involve me?" Edwards requested.

"The song starts with a political figure blowing his mind out in a car. We know the political figure ends up dead in his car." The mayor's face turned ashen while John continued. "You're the biggest political figure that I know, and the only one that has a tie to me. I am suspecting that you will be attacked in your car sometime between now and tomorrow night."

The mayor went quiet and still. From his expression it was obvious that the news that he was the target of a very proficient serial killer had affected him greatly. "When do you think it will happen?"

"Tell me first when your next public appearance will be," John said.

"Tomorrow. The ribbon cutting for the new East Davenport Redevelopment project is at eleven in the morning. After that there is an outdoor luncheon in the center there. It has been in all the papers for months, with greater coverage in the last few weeks. So anyone and everyone knows." The mayor sat back and bit his nail while looking out the window.

Watson stood up. "I know exactly what we'll do. I'll pick you up at your house tomorrow morning at eight. Wear a blue suit, white shirt, and red tie. I will take care of the rest."

John pulled his friend to his feet, hugged him, and strolled out. He had a plan, but no one would know it until the last minute.

Morning came. Moondog picked up the mayor and drove him to his mayoral office. Moses had gone directly to East Davenport to meld with the many city dignitaries preparing for the announcement of the redevelopment project. He saw nothing suspicious and no one that looked like their computer-generated photo of Jerry Jefferson aged. Watson hadn't expected Bungalow Bill, aka "Jelly" Jefferson, to be there, but he wanted to rule it out. It was a few minutes before departure from the government building when Moses gave the all clear. The limo was loaded and pulled away from the building. There would be an attack, but no one knew where.

Five blocks into the trip, a group of protesters against using the funds for economic redevelopment instead of housing for the disadvantaged poured into the street to block traffic. This wasn't a surprise to John Watson. He knew they had gotten a permit to do it just a week before. The protesters were called What's Best for People. As twenty-five protesters shook their signs and shouted, a group of officers surrounded the protesters. Watson believed they were not part of Bungalow Bill's plan.

When the mayor's car entered the block where the protesters were peaceably carrying signs and shouting slogans, Detective Watson realized that he had made a mistake. The protesters slipped up their hoods and pulled pig masks over their faces. The crowd pushed back the barricades and officers, then pressed their way into the street. The mayor's car was rushed, but the cops nearby moved in and forced the protesters, now with their pig masks pulled over their faces, back towards the sidewalk. One of the officers yanked open the rear door, jumped into the seat, and pulled out a gun, pointing it at the mayor. He sang, "He blew his mind out in a car," then followed it with a laugh.

The car's passenger raised his head and whispered in return, "Hello, Jelly. Nice to see you again after all these years."

"Moondog, long time no see." Jerry "Jelly" Jefferson looked into John "Moondog" Watson's eyes. Jerry's face hadn't changed much. There were more lines around the eyes and deep furrows in his brow. He had grown somewhat thinner over the years, but it was still Jelly.

"You're under arrest for murder. Do I need to read off all the victims' names, or will Jean Gilson's be enough?" Watson said as he raised his firearm, pointing it at Jelly.

Jerry giggled. "I guess we are at a stand-off. I have a gun," he said as he rocked it back and forth, then pointed his barrel at Watson's and tapped it. "And you have a gun. You can kill me and I can kill you. Not the way I thought this would play out." He grinned like a man who knew something that no one else knew. "But you don't have one of these." Jerry opened his hand to reveal a radio-controlled detonator. "I push this button and the building we are next to and the protesters I hired all go boom. That means you let me walk out of the car and down the street."

"I can't do that, Jelly," Watson said. "You and I will have to die right here."

"I can't do that, Moondog. I have a body of art work to build, so...."

Jelly pushed the button. An explosion ripped from the second floor of the building, showering glass down on the protesters. John cut his eyes towards the building, the screaming protesters, and the flying debris. He turned back to his nemesis. The door was open and smoke poured into the luxury sedan to replace the maniac that had just so recently filled the seat.

People in black sweatshirts, hoods, and pig masks raced in every direction. The smoke and screams obliterated Watson's view. In the mayhem, Bungalow Bill escaped, as he had planned. It was obvious that the killer had planned this murder attempt and his escape long in advance.

Watson pulled the open door shut, tapped the driver on the shoulder, and told him to drive on. He had missed this chance, but there were several more opportunities. The next time Moondog would look at all escape routes and have them covered as well. The next time he would get the killer. At least this time the intended victim was safe. John pressed a speed dial button for Moses.

"Are you all right, Moonie?" Moses asked as he answered his phone. "We heard an explosion."

"He got away. Jelly was one step ahead of my one step ahead of him. He had planted a bomb to cover his escape. I want you to keep an eye on the mayor, then get him out of there as quickly as possible. I doubt Bungalow Bill will try another attempt on the mayor's life." The sedan pulled up to the celebration. "I'm here now. I will find you, and we will need a long meeting to see what went wrong."

CHAPTER 41

The next song on Moondog's list was "Paperback Writer." John met the two officers covering the event at his recently regular coffee shop. They gave him the details the two had gathered. Officer Ortiz and Officer Grimes placed a floor plan of the Rock Island Library on the table between them.

Ortiz said, "From what the librarian told me, this writer guy, Jake Brandon, is super big right now. He's had a bunch of bestsellers, and his most recent one is going to be made into a movie by Tom Hanks. He is also a native of the area. Went to high school right there in Rock Island. They expect a big crowd. Lots of people will be there." Ortiz pointed to the largest room in the building. "Originally the book reading was scheduled for this room, but if the requests for tickets keep up then they will have to move it to the main hall here." Ortiz stubbed his finger towards the main lobby.

Moondog leaned in close and adjusted his glasses. "If it goes to the main lobby, how will that affect your ability to protect this Brandon guy?"

The tall, blond Officer Grimes sat forward and spoke. "All of a sudden there are more nooks, crannies, and hiding places for a killer to observe from. The metal detector we're putting at the door will keep guns out, but I suspect Bungalow Bill has a way around that. He may not plan on shooting."

"Here is what I want you to do. Get there several hours early. Dress casually. Roam the library and observe everything.

Brandon's reading is at seven, and I will be there by six. I will give you further instructions then." Watson asked the waitress for the bill and the three left.

Moondog needed to go over the lyrics to the song and talk to Jody Johnson about the possible aspects of how to turn a murder in a library into a piece of artwork. He drove towards the Figge as he called her. She was waiting in her office when he walked in. The sunlight was lighting her from behind. She looked more like an angel than an art teacher. She looked up and the lighting shifted. Her desk lamp threw a soft glow across her features.

"I printed out the lyrics to 'Paperback Writer' like you asked. I have some possible ideas." She motioned John to the chair across from her desk. "Look at these lines here." She pointed and John moved closer to read where her finger laid. "Here is the basic concept of the song. This is what's called a query letter. The writer sends his book to a publisher, accompanied by a letter. The letter would be similar to the lyrics. The author says, it is a dirty story. More on the lines of *Fifty Shades of Grey*. His wife doesn't understand him, and he has a son who wants to be a paperback writer, as well."

"No great visual stands out to me. What are you thinking?" Watson asked.

She took a black, felt tip pen from the canister on her desk, reached across the lyrics that laid in front of John, and circled a word—Lear. "This is where we find our visuals. Are you familiar with Shakespeare's play, *King Lear*?"

"In high school I studied Norman Lear, but never *King Lear*. I guess I am about to get the Cliff Notes on that one," Watson responded. Jody caught his wry joke about the man who developed *All in the Family*. Her eyes laughed.

"No Cliff Notes, but I think I can give you the Bungalow

Bill notes. In the song 'I Am the Walrus,' John used clips from a BBC production of *King Lear* at the very end."

"Oh yeah, the 'untimely death' line. That was from *King Lear*?"

"Right, John. As English school boys they most likely were exposed to Shakespeare, and that will be the reason for dropping in the character. The paperback writer in the song had based his book on King Lear, the play." Jody slid back on her chair and smiled. John still looked confused.

"Can you explain further?" he playfully pleaded with his hands folded prayerfully in front of his face.

"The story is simple in some ways and deviously sinister in others. King Lear wanted to pass his kingdom on to his three daughters. My thoughts are that he knew his mind was slipping away. He was making a preemptive strike, since he would be too mad to rule. Basically, he knew he was going mad and was passing his kingdom on to his daughters." Johnson stared at Watson for a moment. "Did Jelly ever have a daughter?"

John thought back to his phone conversation with Jelly. "He said he blamed me for the death of Sexy Sadie, a girl that used to follow the band. He said she died in childbirth. He never said if it was a boy or a girl."

"Alrighty then, it appears to me that the Lear reference is to the play. He may be giving away something here. He knows he is going mad, or maybe there is another health issue. He is turning his kingdom over to his child. I'm betting it is a girl." Jody became quiet. "I wish I had read Jake Brandon's body of work. It is some kind of clash of the clans sort of thing. I only know that because my assistant has read them all, and can't wait for the reading tonight."

"Is she still here? Maybe she can tell us something that

will help," Watson asked.

Jody picked up her phone and dialed her assistant's extension. "Can you come in?"

The assistant answered, "I have about five minutes before I leave for the day."

"That's all it will take."

The college age girl was inside Johnson's office quickly. Jody looked up at her. "I don't want to hold you up, so here is my question. Does the king in the latest Brandon novel kill anyone?"

"That is the point of the book. He goes mad and rains arrows down on his loyal subjects. Finally, his greatest friend and most loyal soldier has to climb the tower and end his life," the girl answered.

"What about his daughter? What happens to her?" Watson asked.

"She tries to protect her father from the hero. Now he has to decide if he has the strength to kill the woman he loves in order to get to the king. All very sad." The assistant turned towards the door while Dr. Johnson thanked her.

"Well, well, it looks like King Lear was the basis for this book as well. Something tells me that arrows will play a part in this murder. Life imitates art once again," she said with a wizened look.

"Thanks, Doctor," Watson said.

"Doctor?" she said as she raised an eyebrow. "Even Batman and Robin were on a first name basis."

"Sorry, my mind is already heading towards the library. I will call you after the reading to tell you how it went," Watson told her as he stood and gathered his notes.

"Are we still on for the gala on Saturday night? I let them know that I have a plus-one joining me," she asked as she stood up and looked at John.

"It is a date," he said. "And no more doctor from me, Jody." He left. He needed to get across the river to the library.

Watson flashed his badge at the door to by-pass the metal detector, and walked into a room already filled with people waiting for the author to show up. Two men had just finished erecting the props that Brandon would use during his reading. John frowned. One whole display was of the weapons used in the three books. His frown grew longer, cutting deep lines into his face when he saw the various bows and arrows. The display would make it easy for Bungalow Bill. The killer may make it to the weapons, but John knew he wouldn't make it out of the library.

He stood in front of the displays and looked carefully. They were authentic, right down the razor-sharp arrow heads.

Ortiz and Grimes walked up behind him. He heard their footsteps and turned his torso to see who was behind him. "We have a problem here, officers," he told them. They both looked at him with puzzled and quizzical faces. "Bungalow Bill will attempt to murder the author using one of these bows. It is your job to stand right here and make sure he cannot get his hands on one of them. Do you understand?" Watson told them with all the authority he had, and they both understood what they had to do.

As Watson pushed his way through the crowd, he saw a face that was not expected. He tapped the woman on the shoulder. "Agent Trew, what brings you out tonight?"

She spun around and a large grin spread across her gorgeous face. "I didn't know you were a fan of the *Clashing Kingdoms* series. If I had known then you could've been my date," she said as she placed her palm on his chest over his heart. He felt the warmth through his shirt. It was a tender touch, but he didn't need the distraction.

"So, Agent Trew, what is your plan for tonight?" John said with a soft smile as he reached up, placing his hand over hers.

"Right now, I will use my fed creds to get me backstage to speak with the author and have him autograph the book. After that I believe I am free for the evening. What do you have in mind, Detective Watson?" she said as her eyes rose to meet his.

She stared. He stared. Watson pulled his hand from hers and her hand from his chest. He didn't want her to feel his heart pumping blood hard and fast. She slid her tongue across her lips and stepped back.

"Like any fan girl, I am here to get an autograph, so please do not distract me with promises of time alone with you," Prudence whispered as she pulled herself away from him and headed towards the door where Jake Brandon, the author, was waiting.

John relaxed. He had two officers near the arrows, and a federal agent with the intended murder victim. He had looked over the crowd, and not one person had any resemblance to Bungalow Bill. That relaxation ended quickly when loud shouting and talking came from the entrance to the library.

A group of a dozen fans pushed their way into the room. Their leader, with a long beard and wearing middle-ages garb, shouted, "We are the *Clashing Kingdoms* fan club, and we are here to listen to the creator of our kingdom, talk about his book. Stand back, peons." The tall man swept aside people in his way with a wide arching movement of his right arm that held a hand-carved staff.

Watson shoved his way to the bearded leader and his eleven followers. He flipped open his credentials and placed them squarely in the tall man's bearded face. He demanded, "Do you have any identification?"

In a booming voice, the leader answered, "Does it look like I have pockets in this tunic? Lighten up, Officer, we're just a simple group of fans out to have a little fun." He held up his hands in a sign of surrender and smiled warmly. "I promise we'll be good." Those around him nodded their heads in agreement. Each wore similar robes. Since the metal detector indicated that no one was armed, John backed off.

"I would appreciate your quiet listening. The author will be on shortly," John said, but he stayed near the group.

At that moment, the director of the Midwest Writing Center moved to the microphone. "Thank you, everyone, for coming out. This is a much bigger turn-out than we expected, but Jake has promised to stay late and sign all your books." The director gave more historical background before introducing the bestselling author.

Jake Brandon walked out to echoing applause. "I am completely overwhelmed by your reception. I can still remember coming to this library and taking out books when I was a small boy. Parents, always remember to encourage reading in your children. Who knows? They could be the next bestselling author. The books I read were a wonderful world for a short, chubby kid to escape into. I suppose I am still escaping into fantasy worlds, only now I have all of you wonderful people to join me." He took a sip of water. "Let me show you some of the props I had commissioned for these readings."

He walked towards the props and held each one up, then told about a scene in one of his books where it was used. As he approached the arrows, John noticed a bit of perplexion on his face. He looked behind the fixture as if he was searching for something. Then he shrugged.

"The last arrow was somehow misplaced, but it is the one used to kill the king at the end of the third book. I am sure it will turn up, but let me read that part of the book to you."

Brandon moved to the lectern where a copy of his book awaited him. He opened the book to the bookmarked page and began reading. The crowd fell silent. To them, these were great words being sung down from the high temple of *Clashing Kingdoms*. John kept his eyes on the bearded leader of the fan club. He watched for any quick movements of his wooden staff. He now knew that an arrow was missing, but there was no bowman in site. He counted the costumed fan club members. There were only eleven of the original twelve that had pushed their way into the grand hall. He looked up and over and around. No bowman in site. He looked up to the balcony—it was empty. His eyes went to the windows of the building and on the doors, searching for reflections. He found what he was looking for.

In a window, he caught the reflection of man in a tunic raising a bow. He was too far back in the doorway to be physically seen, but wasn't aware that his reflection had given him away. Watson shoved hard on the body in front of him to get the guy out of his way. It was a race. He glanced again. The bowman's arrow was notched and the drawstring was pulling back. John pushed harder. People were falling on one another as John pressed harder through the crowd. As John heard the twang of the arrow leaping from the drawstring, he leaped. It was a tackle worthy of his high school football days. He and Jake Brandon went tumbling across the makeshift stage area. Brandon's face looked shocked. He had no idea of what happened until he stared at his arm. His missing arrow had sliced through his shirt, cutting his bicep and then sticking in the wood above his prone body.

People were running for the doors. John looked around for the medieval dressed fan club. They were gone—all had vanished. The crowds were pushing and shoving to get out of the door. It wasn't until the crowd had cleared that John found eleven tunics dropped on the floor. Officers Ortiz and Grimes, along with Agent Trew, made it to the center of the room with him. Watson pointed to the balcony where the arrow had originated. Grimes ran towards the steps to see if anything was there. She got to the top and cautiously entered the room where the shot had come from. She exited and held up a short bow and a tunic.

Watson collapsed to his knees, telling Officer Ortiz to call the station to get a crime scene team on the premises and an ambulance for Jake Brandon. Another killing had been averted, but not by much. Watson was spent. He'd come desperately close to taking the arrow in his back.

Moses had arrived shortly before and raced to Watson. He leaned over his mentor and friend and whispered, "Go home. I will wait for the crime scene investigation team." He paused and pulled his friend to his feet. "Do you have any further instructions for those of us on the scene?"

John shook his head no and headed for the door. He heard running footsteps behind him, and turned to see Prudence Trew jogging up to him. "Are you all right, John?" She placed her hand on his shoulder and gripped tightly. "Do you need someone to go home with you?"

He smiled at her. "Best offer I've had all day, but quite honestly, I just need a drink and then a bed. I have got to get some rest." He turned and grabbed both of her shoulders, looked in her eyes, and said, "And with you, I would get no rest. Go play fan girl and get the writer guy to the hospital."

He squeezed, then released her slowly. Then he walked out.

CHAPTER 42

It was a quiet Friday morning and afternoon at the police headquarters. The captain called him into his office around noon for an update. As he sat, the captain poured out two shots of Jack Daniels and offered one to his head detective. "John, I know you feel like you missed Bungalow Bill, but for the first time we are getting out ahead of the bastard. What's going on? Why are you playing the cards so close to your vest?"

"On the advice of a confidential consultant, I am looking at the killings from a different perspective. I think I know what the next three, or for sure, the next two attempts will be. I am also making sure the left hand doesn't know what my right hand is doing." He looked up and sipped his Jack Daniels.

"Can you tell me why?"

"There is either a bug in our offices or the killer has a mole. I don't know which, so I am playing a game trying to flush out the mole or keep all information from the bug. So far it has worked. Not perfectly, but I'm getting closer," John remarked, then poured the last of his drink down his throat.

"Do you need more back-up? More resources?" the captain asked.

"I want to add another officer for tonight. I'm going to ask Grimes. She performed well last night at the Rock Island Library," Watson said.

"She's a good cop, and I have to say she is tough as nails and cool as the proverbial cucumber. Good choice. I'll authorize her overtime," the captain said, then finished his drink, took John's glass from his hand, and put them back in his locked cabinet.

Watson rose and exited the office. He found Moses and Grimes going over a report on the night before. He slowly walked over. His body was feeling the exhaustion of the last few nights and days. The two cops looked up at Watson and nodded hello. John joined them. "Grimes, I spoke to the captain, and he okayed you joining Moses and I for tonight's stake-out."

"Yes, sir," she responded with a smile. Grimes was tough, but she was also a tall, attractive, lean blonde. She would not attract attention as a cop for this particular mission. Watson motioned for them to walk with him. He led them to the elevator, where he knew it would be a private conversation.

"Lopez and Trew have point on tonight's possible apprehension. I need the two of you to join me outside of the Connections Nightclub around ten thirty."

"Connections? Isn't that the gay nightclub?" she asked. Her face was a scrunched in puzzlement.

"More alternative culture than anything else nowadays. They're having a drag show, and I believe Bungalow Bill is going to attack one of the headliners. It fits with the song 'Get Back.' JoJo is a name used in the song, and a JoJo is performing tonight. It's a perfect scenario for the killer," John said as he leaned on the brick wall outside of the police station. "Dress like you're going out to party. Moses, don't wear anything too slinky," he joked. "Ten thirty tonight. Now go home and get some rest." Watson walked away while the other two headed for the elevator.

The three found each other that night right on time and entered the club. John paid the cover charges for all three—he didn't want to flash a badge. He wore a black leather jacket to hide his service revolver. Sharon Grimes had her gun in her purse, but Moses had brought only his ankle holster pistol. There was no place for him to hide a gun on his tight T-shirt and faded, skin tight jeans.

The place was packed tight and the music thumped hard as Watson, Moses, and Grimes pressed their way slowly past the bar. Moses stopped to buy them all bottles of beer. He knew from experience they were the easiest to carry and to turn into a weapon if needed. Watson had made it to the edge of the tiered dance floor when he heard someone scream out his name. It was Trew on the other side of the dance floor, bouncing up and down, waving her hands to get his attention. The two wove their way through sweaty, half-drunk bodies until they met in the middle.

"I am surprised you came," she said loudly in his ear.

"I heard you talked Lopez into coming in drag, and I had to see it," he said back loudly. Lopez appeared behind her, dressed in his normal, preppy attire, giving his boss a dirty look.

"Nah, he's a real party pooper. I've been protecting him from some of the guys here, though," she said with a laugh. As she spoke a girl moved up behind her and danced with her body rubbing up and down Prudence. Trew ground right back.

"Who's going to protect you?" John joked as he leaned into her ear.

"Who says I want protection?" she laughed, then grabbed John by arm and pulled him towards several tall, round tables crowded by bar stools. "I want you to meet my new friends."

She pulled him in close to the table, and raised her hand to get their attention. "I want you to meet my lover," she yelled. She started the introductions. Most of the names escaped him until she pointed to a very, attractive woman. "This is tonight's star, JoJo Lovelace, and her partner, Michael." John immediately knew why Trew had pulled him over to the table. JoJo was the killer's target for the evening. She was keeping her under surveillance from the perfect spot, right next to her.

Michael reached out his hand and smiled. His short beard didn't hide his good looks or his obvious interest in Prudence's boyfriend. JoJo leaned over and gave John two air kisses on his cheeks. "Why have we never seen any of you at the club before?" JoJo yelled over the pounding dance music.

John shrugged his shoulders. "I guess I'm getting too old for this."

Trew leaned and said, "I like to keep him rested up for other nighttime activities."

The table of people laughed. They could have seen that his face turned red except the dim lights of the club prevented seeing much of anything. The group talked, but Moondog's eyes roamed the room. He saw that Moses and Grimes were sitting with Lopez at another table. Grimes was very close to Moses. Lopez looked more like a third wheel. They were all playing their roles well, except for Moses. He seemed a little too comfortable in his lounge-lizard-lover role.

At eleven, the hostess—a red headed drag star named Ginger—sauntered up to the microphone. "Welcome, everyone. The show is about to begin. Please remember that all of our girls work for tips. Show your appreciation in a practical way. Give them lots of money. To start us off, here is the beautiful and fantastic, Dominique."

The curtains slid open and Dominique charged onto the

stage. She launched into her song and lip-synced to near perfection. Her moves did not reveal any of her masculinity, and convincingly led anyone to believe it was a woman performing. About halfway through her number, John glanced at a flier saying that JoJo was performing next.

Watson leaned into Michael's ear and asked, "Isn't JoJo on next? Shouldn't she be getting ready?"

Michael turned his head and said "The final act canceled. JoJo was moved to the end as the finale, as she deserved. A new girl is performing second." Michael tapped JoJo on the shoulder and asked, "What's that new girl's name?"

JoJo rolled her eyes and flashed her hands in an exaggerated jazz move. "It is the lovely and mysterious Sweet Loretta. Full name is Loretta Hung. You know, like the old movie star, Loretta Young."

It took John a second, but the lines to "Get Back" snapped into his brain. "Sweet Loretta was a man that thought he was woman." The intended target was never JoJo. Bungalow Bill had manipulated the show card and gotten a new performer by the name of Loretta to perform second.

As Dominique ended her song she ran down the center of the aisle to adoring fans, or at least good friends. The curtains had already closed while she was performing. Watson grabbed Michael's arm and showed him his badge. "Listen to me, Michael, I believe a serial killer came here to kill JoJo. I also believe that this new girl will most likely be murdered instead. I need to get backstage now. Can you get me there very quickly?"

Michael didn't wait. He leaped from his chair, pushing people out of his way. The tottering bar goers gave them both dirty looks as the two shoved and jostled their way. Michael was in the lead and Watson was close on his heels when they reached the backstage door. JoJo's partner never let up as he burst through the door.

Watson came in a half second later. Loretta was already strung from a rope thrown over the stage lighting stanchion. The killer held a knife to her throat as he cut from ear to ear, creating a crimson grin running under Loretta's chin. The killer glanced back at Michael and Watson. In one fluid move Bungalow Bill swung his arm and released the knife in a back handed throw. Watson couldn't stop the knife. Instead he launched his body into Michael's, pushing him headlong into the assorted props, but not before the knife embedded itself into Michael's leg.

Right behind Watson came Trew, Grimes, Moses, and Lopez. They watched as Bungalow Bill blew them a kiss and ran from the side room through the curtain slit, down the tiered stage, and out the rear door, untouched and unchallenged.

Grimes dialed her phone to call in the murder as Lopez and Moses moved to cover the two doors. JoJo arrived backstage. Her hands went to her mouth as she saw Sweet Loretta hanging with blood running down her body. Suddenly, her eyes dropped to the floor and saw Michael. The blade of the knife was still sticking out of his leg and into the air. He smiled up at her and shrugged. "You're right, JoJo, you can't take me anywhere without me getting into trouble."

She knelt down beside him and cradled his head. "All these cops, and you decide to be the hero."

The rest of the evening was spent interviewing the people who were in crammed into Connections. As dawn rose over the Mississippi River, Watson led Moses, Lopez, Grimes, and Trew into the street to debrief. "Once again Bungalow Bill was one step ahead of my one step ahead of him. He won tonight. He killed and created a scene. I feel like we failed. I feel like…. Well, I feel like shit, and I'm going home to bed. I advise the rest of you to do the same." He walked towards his car on Second Street. The others did the same. A new day was dawning, but would it be the day that Moondog Watson finally got Bungalow Bill?

CHAPTER 43

Moondog didn't wake until early Saturday afternoon. Still frustrated by the loss of another victim the night before, he moved slowly and angrily towards the coffee pot. He doubled the scoops as he dropped them into the pot. Watson had a philosophy that he existed as three people: Yesterday Moondog, Today Moondog, and Tomorrow Moondog. Yesterday Moondog could care less about Today Moondog. Usually he made the coffee the night before for Tomorrow Moondog. When he got home, he really didn't care what Tomorrow Moondog would think of him. He should have. Today Moondog was tired, grumpy, groggy, and pissed-off. He could have used a little more TLC from Yesterday Moondog. He'd remember to make the coffee tonight for Tomorrow Moondog.

He fell heavily into a kitchen chair as he waited for his jolt of caffeine to drip through. He wasn't a one cupper in the morning, or in this case the afternoon. He would need a pot to just to get near the shower to start his day. Moondog looked at his phone. Moses had called, Jody had called, and Trew had called. He pushed the button for Moses first.

"Yeah," a groggy voice came on the line.

"Why'd you call? I was trying to sleep," Moondog said into the phone.

"If you would have listened to your voice mail, you would know I was telling you not to call me. I was sleeping, but now

I am awake. Anything new?" Moses said as grumpily as his mentor.

"Waiting for the coffee to drip through so I can wake up," he answered, paused, and started again. "I can't believe that Jelly Jefferson outsmarted us again."

"Me, either."

"Something bothers me though. The whole switch to a new performer happened late yesterday. Find out who the original show closer was and drop by their place. Find out how that one went down. Bungalow Bill may have already knocked her off. Take Lopez and Grimes with you," John said.

"Can I skip Lopez and just take Grimes?" Moses joked.

"Moses, keep your mind in the game."

"She looked hot in street clothes. What do you expect out of a red-blooded male?" Moses answered.

"You better skip Grimes and just take Lopez," Moondog joked. He waited a beat before continuing. "Have Grimes at the front door and send Lopez around to the back. The show closer could even be in on it."

"Right, boss," he answered. "What are you up to tonight?"

"I'm chasing down the 'Baby, You're A Rich Man' hunch. Big, black tie, gala thing with Dr. Johnson," Moondog answered.

"Maybe Lopez should go with you so you'll keep your head in the game," Moses laughed.

"I am falling on the floor laughing, Moses. Listen, my coffee is done. I need the pick-me-up. Let me know what you find."

Moondog hung-up and rose from the chair. His body ached. He was truly ready for retirement. He had managed to stay in good shape for his whole career, but these last few weeks had aged him and caused new aches and pains to blossom in his body.

While drinking his first cup of coffee, John dialed Dr. Johnson. After niceties, he asked, "What time am I picking you up?"

"Starts at seven, and his galas are not designed for the fashionably late. So, can you be here at six thirty?"

"Yeah, I should be awake by then," Moondog grumbled into the phone.

"I read the story in the paper. Bad night and morning, huh?"

"Real bad. I've got to catch Bungalow Bill tonight. Who knows how many people he plans to kill, or even how he plans to do it?"

"We don't, and I see no clues in the song," she answered.

"We can listen to it on the way and see if something pops out at both of us. Gotta go. See you tonight."

Moondog hung up and grabbed another cup of coffee. He went to his stereo system and pulled the stereo version of "Baby, You're A Rich Man" from the album rack. He dropped the needle into the groove and turned up the volume. There had to be a clue in the lyrics. It was originally two songs that John and Paul mashed together. The "Beautiful People" referred to San Francisco's Haight Ashbury hippies. It was the Summer of Love, and this was the formation of the rock 'n' roll, drugs, and free love generation. John would be hanging out with the "beautiful people" of the Quad Cities. It would be a crowd of rich men and rich women, but he didn't believe that Bungalow Bill would be looking back on the Summer of Love. He wanted to grind John Watson's reputation into the ground.

He sat listening to the song. It was Paul's section of the lyrics that finally caught his ear. The rich man kept all his money in a brown bag. He was ready to formulate a plausible plan when his phone rang again. It was Trew.

"How are you doing today, John?" she asked.

"Tired and frustrated."

"Me, too. Need some company?" she asked, but without a hint of flirtation.

"Would love it, but I have a dinner to attend and I can't get out of it. Let's make plans for tomorrow. Tell you what, let's make a day of it. Dinner out, a walk by the river, then dessert at my place," Moondog offered.

"You're on, Moondoggie. That will be exactly what Dr. Robert ordered," she said quickly, and with a reference to a Beatles song tied to it. "See you around five, but where?"

"There is an outdoor café in East Davenport on the street where you come in. Five is good. We can lick our wounds," he said, then added, "among other things." They both laughed and hung up. John grabbed another cup of coffee and walked towards the shower. He smiled to himself. He was confident that this ordeal was coming to an end.

CHAPTER 44

Moondog pulled up in front of Jody Johnson's house. She pulled her door open and walked out, but he met her halfway up the walk. She tossed her keys at him while saying, "We better take my car. Somehow I don't think a Crown Vic with no hubcaps would fit in."

"It screams cop, doesn't it?" he said with an embarrassed smile.

"From a mile away,"

"Won't people recognize me from all the pictures in the paper lately?" he asked.

"Keep the sunglasses on, Hollywood. The monkey suit looks good on you, and is a good distraction. You should pass as a moderately rich guy," she joked while the two walked towards her Audi.

Once on the road, she touched his hand while it rested on the gear shift. "Have you given the song lyrics any thought?" she asked as her hand closed around his.

"Not much there. We know he was a big game hunter, but I don't think he keeps his money in a big, brown bag. I believe we'll know more after we see the mansion."

They were silent for a few minutes, then Jody asked a question to fill in the dead air. "Did you get to the Magical History Tour when it was at the Putnam?"

"The Moondogs played the opening night. Did you go?" John said.

"So, you were the cute guy in the band that I kept staring at all through dinner? I should have put two and two together," she said with a smile that warmed him inside. "What did you think of the exhibit?"

"I think I looked at the exhibits from a totally different perspective. I nearly peed myself when I saw Colin Hanton's Quarry Men drum set. That was all pre-Beatles, even pre-McCartney. I wanted to touch it and play it. You know, the Quarrymen are still playing together as a band, but two of them have died," John started to rattle on. "Then to see the Cavern Club rebuilt stage to the exact dimensions of the original — I was absolutely blown away." John's face beamed. He looked like a boy talking about his first Christmas. "I'm sorry, I kind of ran away with the conversation. What impressed you the most?"

"I loved seeing the photos. You could see the hysteria of the fans caught in their faces. I almost felt as if I was there with them. The Avedon photos were exquisite. I sometimes think we forget what great artists ended up surrounding the Beatles." She was beaming as she spoke as well. "What one memory did you take away from the show?"

"The most emotional moment was when I saw the Double Fantasy album that John signed for Mark David Chapman," he responded without a second's thought.

"Yeah, me too. What's the story behind the album? How did they find it?" she asked.

"According to the legend, Chapman set it in a tree. After he shot Lennon it fell from the tree into a flower planter beneath it. A guy found it, turned it in as evidence, and then got it back. The last sales price I heard for the album was $525,000, but that was 2003. Gotta be worth a lot more now. I'm glad it was in the show. I'm glad it is impacting people the way the original murder affected me."

John ended his story as the two pulled up to the Charles Davenport estate. When Moondog looked around at the cars parked along the long circular drive, he realized that Jody was right. His Crown Vic would have stood out among the Mercedes, Rolls, BMWs, and Volvos. Once parked, the two hiked towards the mansion, then entered the home before being directed to the garden party in the back by the pool. As they walked through the grand foyer, John noticed the display for the charity event.

Cans of food built a sizable pyramid. The charity was for World Hunger, and sitting on top of the cans was a large, brown grocery bag with a sign that said, "Place Your Donations Inside the Bag." The bag appeared to be protected by several stuffed heads of various beasts with overly aggressive sneers. He tugged on Jody's hand and pointed. "Here's the bag sitting in the zoo, but it gives us no clues as to what is going to happen."

"Let's go to the party, and maybe something will jump out at us," she said as she pulled him by the hand to the back-yard gardens, pool, and the party-goers.

The mayor caught Watson out of the corner of his eye. He waved and called John and Jody over to his group. He introduced John, who introduced Jody Johnson to the group. The men in the group were discussing Iowa State's chances at a winning schedule. Keesha noticed Jody's eye glaze over during the football talk. In an ever present, graceful, and beautiful movement, she led her away towards the bar. With glasses of white wine in their hands, the ladies found a garden bench and sat down.

"Tell me how you know Johnny?" Keesha asked as a conversation starter.

"I had a unique take on his latest case," Jody answered.

"Tell me, tell me," Keesha coaxed excitedly.

"I am an art history professor at the Figge, and an assistant curator. I thought I saw something in the recent rash of killings that reminded me of an artist I had heard of. We talked, and I guess we sort of clicked," Jody said between sips of wine.

"John was married to my best friend, Jesse, for several years, but Jesse, like most cop's wives, could not take the hours, and the fear of him not coming home, any longer. John and Mark stayed friends. I actually dated John myself for a while before he introduced me to Mark. After that, it is political history." She tipped the glass and drank down the last inch of her wine. "Are you guys serious?"

"This is actually our first date. Well, kind of a first date. He is on the job, and I am his cover for being here. We're not serious, but...."

"But what?" Keesha stopped and flashed her bright grin. It was the type of smile that won hearts and votes. "I get it. You wish it were serious. He is wonderful man, so I don't blame you." She paused again, then said, "And quite good looking." They both laughed. "It will be our secret until that knucklehead catches on. When it comes to romance, that guy exists without a clue."

The two women were interrupted by the party's host taking the stage where the band was playing. He spoke into the microphone. "Ladies and gentlemen, may I have your attention." The crowd quieted. "As many of you know, I have been fortunate enough to travel the world. I have looked into the eyes of many children, and have seen their despair and hopelessness. I have seen children without a thing. I have seen the ravages of hunger firsthand.

"Those of us here are surrounded by wealth, good health,

good fortune, and an abundance of food. On my last trip to India I decided I had to do something about those hungry children. I started the World Hunger Initiative to do one thing—feed the children." He raised the over-sized grocery brown bag and said, "In a few moments, my executive director of the World Hunger Initiative, Brittany Winters, will make her way through the crowd to you as you enjoy the music and food. As she goes by please drop a generous gift into the bag. Once she has made it through all of you, then we will announce a tally. Please give from the heart. Please give all that you can." He gave the microphone over to his young, very attractive executive director.

"I will start walking through the crowd in a few moments to give you enough time to dig deep in those Michael Kors' purses and the pockets of your tuxedos. Help us feed the children." She set the microphone back in the stand and picked up the grocery bag. She moved through the crowd accepting checks from the many beautiful people at the party. As she did it, the band started to play once again.

Jody walked up next to Watson and slipped her arm into his. "I'm starving. Let's grab something to eat." The two walked towards the overflowing buffet. "Where do you think he will attack?"

"If I knew who the target was then this would all be easier. Mr. Davenport would be a big enough kill, but he will be surrounded by friends and admirers all night. Any ideas from the conceptual art perspective?" he asked.

"None at all. But tell me, how are you going to deal with the situation if Bungalow Bill is able to pull off another murder?" she asked as they filled their plates with food.

"He's beaten me before, but a loss here will put my reputation in the crapper. I don't have the option to lose," he answered after taking a long breath.

"Then think like him. You know more about the Beatles than he does. Put your mind inside his head. Become him," Jody encouraged.

John stopped where he stood. He sang the song in his head. He went over the history of the song. He looked at the "beautiful people" and the money kept in a big, brown bag inside the zoo of stuffed animal heads. It hit him.

"Jody, it is not a coincidence. The big brown bag is not a coincidence. Whoever came up with that idea is tied to Bungalow Bill. He or she is either in on it or they will be the target. I'm betting on that executive director girl."

John set his full plate down on a table and moved quickly through the crowd, searching for the young lady holding the bag. Although he was moving quickly, she seemed to have already made it through the people and had disappeared.

He moved towards the house and the main foyer, where the bag had originally sat. She wasn't there, but the bag had not yet been returned to the top of the mountain of food cans. He turned around and went to the back porch and the steps down to the garden and pool. Moondog's eyes roamed from side to side. Finally, he saw her making her way across the yard to the well-over three thousand square foot pool house.

Watson took the steps two at a time, then broke into a sprint across the manicured, grassy lawn towards the pool house. The seconds ticked off in his head. Bungalow Bill would be there waiting. He would kill her, and somehow make it gruesome enough to create a distinct frenzy among the people. John ran harder as the crowd of puzzled people watched him race towards the pool house.

He pushed the door open with the weight of his body. The young woman lay on the floor face down. He saw the last of a figure run out the back door. More importantly, he saw Bungalow Bill, aka Jelly Jefferson, leaning over the young woman with a samurai sword held high over his head.

Watson already had his gun in his hand when he yelled, "Put down the weapon or I shoot right now!"

Jelly straightened up and dropped the sword. He smiled at John as if it was simply two old friends bumping into each other on the street. "Hey. Why, if it isn't my old childhood friend, Moondoggie. You kind of caught me in the middle of something," Jelly said as he motioned down at the unconscious woman on the floor. Then he glanced at his watch. "Could you come back a little later? Say fifteen minutes or so?" Jelly said as he grinned and took a step towards John.

"Stay where you are. Get down on the floor with your hands behind your head. You are under arrest," Watson barked.

"Déjà vu all over again, Johnny. You catch me. You say you're going to arrest me, and then it happens. I walk away," Jelly said softly and calmly.

"Not this time, Jelly," John said just before the front door burst open.

Two security guards raced inside. Not knowing who was who and that John was a cop, one tackled him. His gun went skidding along the marble floor. Before the other guard could make it to Bungalow Bill, he was running for the back door. John heard a dirt bike start up as Bill hit the door. Then he heard the engine race off.

John pulled in a breath and told the guard to look in his coat pocket for his badge. Once the man found it, he got off of Watson and apologized.

John looked at him and shook his head. "You just let a serial killer get away, you friggin' idiot." He pushed himself to his feet and walked over to the woman. He felt for a pulse. She was alive. Watson pulled out his phone and called the police station. "Send an ambulance and a black and white to the Charles Davenport Estate. The injured person is in the pool house." He moved to his service revolver, picked it up, and re-holstered the weapon.

The two guards were told to stay with the girl before Watson walked outside. The first person he saw was Jody. She hugged him like she never wanted to let go. The second face was the mayor's, and the third was Charles Davenport's, looking more puzzled than anyone had ever seen him before. John pulled the men inside the pool house. "Just tell everyone that I prevented a robbery and that everything is safe."

"What is the real story, Detective?" the mayor asked.

"Bungalow Bill was thwarted by Quad Cities finest, but he escaped thanks to the intervention of the two security guards inside." Watson jerked his eyes with derision towards the two embarrassed men. "An ambulance is coming to take the lady to the hospital. I am arresting her later under suspicion of collaborating with Bungalow Bill. Mayor, please fill Mr. Davenport in. I need to wait for my black and white to give them instructions. I also have a plate of food waiting for me, and a lovely woman to escort me to the table," Moondog said, then took two steps away before turning back and adding, "And I believe there is a tall Jack and Coke with my name on it."

As he walked away with Dr. Johnson, she grabbed his arm tightly and leaned into his ear, "You sure know how to show a girl a good time." He laughed, then laughed harder. She followed suit.

CHAPTER 45

John Watson and Jody Johnson returned to her car after the party broke up. Most people believed the robbery story and had gone back to enjoying the party. Once it ended, John and Jody left and drove in silence. As he parked her car, John slipped from the driver's side and ran around to open Johnson's door. Her tanned legs slid through the side slit of her long dress. John looked. He was starting to like everything about this woman.

"Thanks, Mr. Hero. I have to admit that you really know how to show a girl a good time. It was a wonderful evening for me, even though you didn't capture the bad guy. Definitely the most interesting date in my lifetime," she said while staring into his warm, passionate eyes. She wondered what she would say if he asked to come in. It would be hard to say no, but her internal guidance system had always said it wasn't a good move on the first date, even if it was a cover for his sleuthing.

John stared back into her eyes. He stumbled over his words, sucked in a breath, and finally got them out. "I truly enjoyed my time with you. Sorry it turned into a night of catching or not catching bad guys. We need to get together after this is all over. I owe you a nice evening out." He paused. His eyes turned away from hers, then he glanced back. "I have a long day tomorrow. I better get going," he said as he dropped her keys in her hands.

They hadn't moved. The two were still inches apart. She wanted him to kiss her. He wanted to kiss her. He stammered again like a schoolboy after the teen dance, "Would it be all right if I…? Well, if we…. I mean, if — "

She didn't wait for the words to finally come out. Standing on her tiptoes, her mouth mashed against his. It was a long kiss, a kiss that they both wanted to have happen. As the two broke, both their faces looked more like teenagers that had kissed for the first time. It would be a kiss that both of them would remember.

John stumbled backwards ungracefully and almost lost his balance. Jody giggled at his near fall. He exaggerated with his arms extended outward like a tight rope walker in a more careful walk backwards towards his car. Jody walked to her door, turned and smiled, unlocked the door, and went inside. John waited until she was safe, started his car, and drove home. John touched his lips a few times as he drove, and smiled. He liked this intelligent, attractive woman. His dreams that night were pleasant, and he woke up the next day smiling.

Later in the morning, he arrived at his office in faded blue jeans and an untucked shirt. He made a call to the front desk to find out where Brittany Smith, the Executive Director of the World Hunger Initiative, had been taken. The hospital had kept her overnight for observation. By now, Brittany would have realized that she had been set-up. Watson drove to the hospital and walked to her room.

The woman looked up at him as he entered. "I'm Detective Watson. Is it all right if I ask a few questions?" She looked up at him and stood to reach out her hand. Even in a hospital gown and a bandage on her head, John could tell she was beautiful woman that knew how to use her sexuality to gain what she wanted.

"I don't think we've met, Detective," Brittany said. "I understand that you saved me from the robbers killing me."

John smiled and sat down, motioning for Winters to do the same thing. "Ms. Winters, you don't have to play the game for me. I know that you had previous contact with your attacker. How else would he know your movements? I also believe that he gave you the idea for using the big, brown bag. So let's cut to the quick. How did he approach you?"

She feigned shock, but it was poor acting. John sat back and waited. He finally leaned forward. "Just so you know, the killer will attempt to murder you again. He doesn't like loose ends. He tried to kill you once and will make another attempt. I am your only salvation."

Brittany's eyes filled up with tears. She knew he was right. "You're right. I met Mr. Jefferson a few months back. Although he was a few years older than me, I was seduced by his charm. We've been sleeping together for several weeks now. He came up with the idea and plans for the whole gala event, and the brown bag idea."

She was crying and reached for the tissue box near her bed. "We were going to steal all the money and run off together. I was so in love with him, I am embarrassed to say. My adoration ended when he struck me. In a daze I thought I heard him say he was going to kill me."

"Was there someone else in the pool house with him?"

Brittany closed her eyes and thought for a moment. She opened them and spoke. "I only saw a figure in the shadows."

"Man or woman?" He asked.

"I didn't see, but got the impression that it was a woman," she answered. "Then I was struck. That is all I remember."

"Thank you for telling the truth. I will do what I can to

get you a lighter sentence," said John as he stood to leave the hospital room.

"Are you saying that I am going to jail?"

John looked back over his shoulder and said, "If you can't do the time then don't do the crime." He walked out of the room listening to her sobs.

Once in his car he called Moses. He wanted him, Lopez, and Grimes to meet him at the coffee shop. Once they had settled in, John told them about the night before. He had a plan for the next song, which he believed would be, "Come Together," and their last attempt to capture Bungalow Bill. He laid out his plan and revealed key clues about the killer. His reveal stunned them all, but his trail of evidence convinced them that Moonie was probably right. The three left their boss and went back to the station to prepare his plan.

It was mid-afternoon, and the skies were clouding over the blue sky. The air didn't feel like rain yet. His date with Prudence Trew would still be at the patio café. He called her to make sure their plans were still on.

"Dinner at five still?" he asked.

"Absolutely. I have a lot to say to you, Moonie," she answered excitedly.

"Like what, Pru?" he answered with a quizzical tone in his voice.

"To begin with, I put in for a transfer to this office. I feel like we are just starting the best relationship I've ever had. I want to give it some time to blossom and grow. Is that all right with you?"

He paused before he spoke. "Wow, that is great news, but you realize that I am a good eighteen years older than you. I'll soon be a retired, old cop kicking around the house, bored to death, and cranky like old cops get. That's what you're getting yourself into."

"John, I want to spend the rest of my life with you. When we have dinner, I want to talk about what all that will look like. After dinner can we go back to your place and celebrate? I really need you today," she said in a way that made him absolutely sure of what she meant.

"I think I can work a night of good love into my schedule," he laughed, and the two hung up their phones.

CHAPTER 46

John sat at a table nearest the sidewalk in the hip, village of East Davenport. Baked was a new restaurant, but was attracting many of the counter culture and wealthier patrons. He sipped a tall glass of fresh þrewed ice tea as he waited for Agent Prudence Trew. He glanced at his watch for the tenth time. It was a quarter past five. She was late. In his experience with her, she was never late. John Watson sighed. From what Trew had said, she wanted the two of them to work on a more permanent relationship. His mind thought through the last several days, and then settled on Dr. Jody Johnson. Something stirred inside of him when he thought of her. He felt conflicted, and that meant that he would have to make a decision unless her lateness was a sign that a decision had already been made.

He glanced at his watch again. It was twenty after, and still no Prudence Trew. His phone rang. He smiled. It was probably Trew telling him she was on her way. But it wasn't. He answered the phone and heard a song float out of the speaker. It was as he'd suspected the next song would be, "Come Together."

Right on cue, a young black man wearing jeans, a gray Sgt. Pepper's T-shirt, and a long coat made from a shaggy material that hung to his knees, skated up to the railing next to John. The detective reached for his gun, but all the young man had in his hands was an MP3 player and ear buds. John took them from him, then looked at the boy's head. He wore his thick hair in a high, severe flat top haircut, right in line with the song on Watson's phone. "Here come old flat-top with hair down to his knees," John thought. The boy walked away to a smooth groove song playing somewhere inside his head.

Watson turned off his phone and placed the ear buds into his ears. He pushed the play button. The song was an older Beatles favorite of his, "You're Going To Lose That Girl." Lennon sang it in a huskier voice. His first thought went to Jody, but the obvious reference was to the woman he was intending to have dinner with, Prudence Trew. In the middle of the song was an edit. It was the sound effect of a needle skipping across a record until it landed on a new song. Paul's voice sang out "Penny Lane." At first Watson tried to meld the two songs together, but seconds later he realized it was a message and a location. The message was that Bungalow Bill held Prudence captive, and it was on Penny Lane. He knew there was no Penny Lane in the Quad Cities, but there was a Lincoln Avenue, often called Penny Lane by his group, the Moondogs. John rose from the table, dropped a five-dollar bill on it, then walked towards his car. He was smiling. The ordeal was about to come to an end. The question in his mind was, who would walk out alive?

CHAPTER 47

There was no number given for Lincoln Avenue, but he knew that Bungalow Bill would make the building recognizable. Watson drove Lincoln from near the North Park Mall towards the river. With each block Lincoln diminished in its values. He hit a block that had been primarily businesses and light industrial buildings. Ahead on the street was a five-story, decaying structure. On the fifth floor he saw dim lights. Watson pulled to a stop five structures away from the building. The old building had a new sign attached, sporting the German word, Kaiserkeller. John smirked. That was the name of the hole in the wall night club where the Beatles, along with Pete Best, had hammered out their rock 'n' roll sound. It was in a rough, seedy part of Hamburg, Germany.

John moved to the trunk of his car and pulled out a bag he had prepared, just in case this scenario ever happened. He opened the bag and pulled out what he needed. He approached the building, keeping close to the wall to hinder detection. Watson found the front door open, which told him that it wasn't the way to go in. Cutting through the alley, he found a rear door. He quietly pried the lock from the door and moved stealthily through the filth lying on the floor. His pen light gave him enough illumination to see, but not enough light to be detected. He found the metal and cement steps and went up slowly. He smiled—no creaks to give him away.

Watson climbed slowly, checking behind him and

checking ahead of him. He wanted to assure himself that he wasn't walking into a trap of his own making. On the fourth floor he heard music playing on the floor above. It seemed that Bungalow Bill wasn't expecting him as of yet. That was good. He climbed slowly and carefully, then crossed the hallway to a closed door. He heard the music inside and two people talking. His time was now to show who had been the hunter and who was being hunted.

Watson pulled his phone from his pocket and a small MP3 player. He dialed Trew's phone. He could hear it ring inside the room.

"Answer it. It must be lover boy Johnny Moondog. I bet he got lost, the frigging idiot," Jelly Jefferson said.

"I doubt he got lost. The guy is cautious," Trew said as she pushed the button on her phone, "John, help me. He's going to kill me," she screamed into the phone. She expected to hear Watson's angry voice come back at her. Instead, John pushed the button on his MP3 player and sent a song over the phone line.

"Tell Me Why" was an angst filled tune that asked the woman in the song why she lied to the singer. Watson could hear it inside. He smiled. Only he knew what was coming next.

Trew yelled to Bungalow Bill, "He figured it all out. We need to get out of this place now. He'll have it crawling with cops in a few minutes."

With his suspicions answered, Watson put a big, solid boot into the door near the knob. It went flying open and the figure of John "Moondog" Watson loomed big in the doorway, holding a pistol and a very illegal sawed-off shotgun. Watson had a big smile on his face as he called out Jack Nicholson's famous line from *The Shining*, "Here's Johnny!"

Jelly made a move for the automatic pistol on the table in front of him, but John whistled at him. "No, no, no. This time we aren't going to have a stand-off. This time the good guy wins." He looked at Trew sitting in a high-backed stool, swiveling his way. She was not tied. She was not chained. She was simply holding her phone with a shocked and surprised look on her face. "Hello, Prudence. Sorry you missed our date. I had planned to break it off with you tonight over dinner, but I guess I can do it right here and right now. Are you ready for the big let-down?" He paused before barking out, "It's over, you lying bitch." Then John smiled and turned back to Jelly.

"Jerry Jefferson, you are under arrest for multiple murders. You have the right to remain silent. Anything you say can and will be used against you in a court of law. You have the right to speak to an attorney, and to have an attorney present during any questioning. If you cannot afford a lawyer, one will be provided for you at government expense."

Jelly smiled back at John. "We've gotten to this place a few times before, Moondoggie. Each time, I get away. This time won't be any different, but I do have a question for you, my old buddy, Moonie. I knew you would eventually figure out who I was, but how did you figure out who Prudence was?"

"I've known since 'Maxwell's Silver Hammer.' I had admired her perfume, *Have Mercy*. It was distinctive. When I walked into the judge's chambers that morning, the faint scent of it still lingered, and yet she hadn't gone in the room during the crime scene investigation," he said as he kept an eye on both of them. "I called Erica, who made it. I described Trew to her, and she described the woman's father to me. Amazingly, she described someone who looked a lot like you, my old school friend, Jelly Jefferson.

"She made another mistake when she overheard me with the doctor about the move of Jean Gilson. She claimed she had just gotten there. I'm a suspicious guy. I went and got the surveillance tape, and guess what I saw? The surveillance tape showed that she listened, then sent a text before walking in." Watson smiled. He had more to say, but he knew that talking would only give Jelly time to come up an escape plan. He had seen it too often in the movies. This wasn't a movie.

Jelly began a slow move of his hands down from over his head. John motioned with the barrel of his gun for Jelly to put them back up. "The killing of Officer McCarren was a dead give-away, since Trew had heard me praise her. It was a bit of revenge for Prudence. I could go on and on. She left a constant trail, and I stayed vigilant."

Watson found himself a chair and sat down while keeping his pistol on Jelly and the shotgun on Trew. "You were the biggest idiot, Jelly. That whole *Stench of Death* art show using Pete Best's given name Scanland was fairly stupid. You most likely did that before conceiving this killing spree of yours. You left clues like that all through your life. You're really not as smart as you think, and you were a God-awful, lousy drummer."

At the last comment, Jefferson took a step forward. John put a bullet in the wooden beam next to his head. The killer stopped. John turned his head towards Trew. "You probably already know that Jelly here is your real father. By the way, you look a lot like your mother. Dave Gettings caught that and drew my attention to it. It didn't take me long to find that Sexy Sadie had a daughter that would be your age." John was ready to deliver the hardest blow of all. "Jelly, here, gave you up for adoption, then when he was ready to groom you, he murdered your good, loving parents. Didn't know that, did

244

you?"

The surprise, shock, and anger flashed across her face. She stared at Jefferson with fire in her eyes.

Jelly stammered out, "That's not true."

"Sorry, Jelly, I gave the Boston P.D the information I had on that case. They've reopened that cold one, and you will most likely ride the needle for that if Iowa doesn't put you to death first." He grinned at Jelly and said, with a bit of mockery in his voice, "Wow, this is turning into a really bad day all around for you, isn't it?"

"I still plan to walk out of here, Moonie," Jelly said, but this time his smile had gone from his face. Jelly's eyes danced around the room, searching for a way out or a distraction.

"Don't know how, Jelly," John calmly stated. "Trew, go to the window and look outside. Tell Daddy what you see."

She got up slowly and backed to the window. She stared down. She turned around with her face dropping into a worried frown. "There are cop cars everywhere. The building is surrounded," she said gloomily. Then she turned to John. "He brainwashed me. He forced me to help him. I've been a fool to follow him. Help me get out of this. I really do love you, Johnny."

"All that may get you out of the death penalty," Watson said.

She opened her arms and walked towards John with tears rolling down her face. Watson shook his head and laughed at her. She screamed at him and took another step in his direction. Watson aimed the shotgun into the ceiling and discharged it. She went motionless.

The distraction was all that Jelly Jefferson needed. He snatched a bottle of liquid from the table in front of him. "Don't shoot, John," the killer said. "This is a highly volatile accelerant. A shot would spill it, and this old tinderbox will go up in flames faster than we could get out. We would all die, and I don't think dying in some inferno is how you want to start retirement. Just let us walk out of here, and I promise to stop and once again become a model citizen." Bungalow Bill held up his fingers in the scout's honor symbol.

"Nice offer, Bungalow Bill, but I already have firetrucks on standby. This time I figured out all the possible escape routes, and this time I have them covered. Put the bottle down and I'll put a nice set of cuffs on you, so you can go to jail. It's all over, Jefferson. It is all over."

As John finished talking Jelly raised his arm and dropped the bottle. Watson hadn't expected that. John raised his weapon at the same time and shot the bottle. It burst into flames and the liquid drenched over Bungalow Bill. He was a fireball in a second. Screaming in pain, the killer raced down the hallway behind him. John shot two more times, certain that one of the bullets struck the madman's back, but the maniac kept running. He turned the bend and the screams turned to echoing agony that moved quickly away, fading into a descent into an open elevator. They stopped abruptly and a bone crushing thud was heard.

Watson raced down the hall through a rivulet of flames that grew up as the accelerant had dropped from Jefferson's body. John stopped short of the open elevator shaft. He stared down as a ball of hot flames consumed the body below. John radioed Moses, "The bandit is at the bottom of the elevator shaft."

"We're outside the door. Coming in." The room's door popped open. Moses, Lopez, and Grimes burst in. John looked over to where Trew had last been standing. She was gone.

"Where's Trew?" he yelled. The flames were growing in

the room.

"She didn't come out our way. There has to be a secret exit or escape route," Moses yelled.

Grimes pressed against the walls looking for a false wall. When she turned, the flames were dancing along the floor. She screamed to the others, "We need to get off this floor and out of here now. The flames are reaching the ceiling."

The four hopped the stairs down two at a time. As they broke into the open air wheezing from the smoke, John looked up to see the roof explode into flame. Jelly Jefferson was dead, but Prudence Trew, he was sure, had escaped.

Chapter 48

For two hours the firemen fought the blaze. Watson had the cops pull their perimeter back a block to allow the four companies of fire departments the room they needed to douse the flames. On the right side of the building was another abandoned building. It was too close to prevent damage, but the fire did not destroy the entire building in either case. The firetrucks' quick arrival prevented complete damage to either building.

As dawn came, the firemen wound up their hoses. Inspectors moved in and out of the buildings, and finally gave the all clear for the medical examiner's office to secure the charred remains from the elevator.

As they wheeled out the body, Watson was next to them. "Do we have much left of the corpse?" he asked.

"Enough to get an identification, eventually. There isn't much left of his remains, but I do have a skull and it does have teeth. That's how we'll identify him. Not much left to see. If you go inside, be careful. This structure will have to come down. I don't think it's safe. Scared the crap out of me, going inside." The medical examiner told his men to get the body back to the morgue. He looked again at Watson and smiled. "It appears that you got him, Detective. Congratulations. Now you can finally retire."

The medical examiner reached out a hand to John. They shook. Watson wasn't as confident that the whole ordeal was over. Bungalow Bill may be dead, but like in Shakespeare's *King Lear*, he had wished to pass his kingdom on to his daughter. No evidence had been found of her body so far. He smiled at the examiner. He wasn't confident that the ordeal was completely over, but it was finished for now.

He walked over to Moses, Lopez, and Grimes. The three were leaning on a black and white, sipping coffee brought in by one of the cops. Moses raised a Styrofoam cup to Moonie and handed it to him. He asked, "What did the medical examiner say?"

"He'll be able to get an ID off the dental records. Not much left of Bungalow Bill. That wasn't the way I wanted it to go down, but as a coach says, a W is a W." He raised his coffee cup in a salute to his partners. "Lopez and Grimes, you two can go home. Moses and I need to walk the remains of the buildings with the inspectors. After that we all go home and go to bed."

Watson turned around to see the mayor and the police captain shaking hands with the firemen and policemen near them. The two walked together towards Watson. "Did you get him, Moonie?" asked the mayor.

"The medical examiner has to confirm it, but I believe this one is over," Watson said, smiling and reaching out to take their hands.

"How did you finally solve this one, Moondog?" Captain Roudebush asked.

"It will all be in the report, which will be on your desk in roughly two days. I am taking tomorrow off, and I gave those three over there the day off as well." He pointed to Moses, Lopez, and Grimes.

The captain nodded, smiled, and then said, "My money is on the three of you showing up tomorrow anyway just to bask in the win. Especially Moses. Sammy Moses has taken on more of your characteristics than I had hoped for. He'll be a good lead detective." Captain Roudebush took John's shoulder and asked in a low tone, "Should I promote Grimes? You counted on her a lot in the last few days."

"Yeah, make her the Wonder Woman to Batman and Robin over there," he laughed.

The captain gave a rare smile. Moses was already moving towards Moondog when the captain caught him. After his job well done talk with Moses, Moses moved to a position next to Watson. They waited for the fire inspectors to take them on a tour.

"What am I looking for, Moonie?" Sam Moses asked.

"Trew got away. I can feel it. There had to be a way to cross from one building to the other. On the Kaiserkeller building there is a back staircase running along that side of the building." He pointed it out. "If she got down to a lower floor, then she might have had a way to cross over to the other building. If she got there, then she could have slipped out of the other building then down the alley. Make sure you check the alley for a thick, wide plank that could have stretched between the two buildings. I want to know how she escaped," Watson said.

A moment later the inspectors led the two through the buildings. Nothing was found that would make anyone suspect that one of the killers had gotten away. John's hunch was unsubstantiated, but he still felt he was right. He could feel it.

CHAPTER 49

"It's been a month since you stopped Bungalow Bill, and two weeks since you retired. How do you like being a shopkeeper?" Jody asked as she unfolded her napkin at the Faithful Pilot restaurant on the shore of the Mississippi River. John was staring out the window at the riverboat Twilight. He wanted to take a day cruise with Jody in the near future. He wanted the two of them to get away, even for a few hours. "Johnny, did you hear me?"

"I did, but I was thinking about the riverboat. Have you been on it?"

"No, but are you asking if I'd like to? The answer is yes," she said with a smile.

"Good. When?"

"You make the plans and I'll take the time off," she answered.

"Back to your question. I must admit that I miss the excitement of my former profession, but being able to devote myself to the shop is good for me. I also started booking the Moondogs for more gigs." He paused, then nearly spit out the water he was sipping. "The local rock station wants me to do a two-hour Saturday morning show called the 'Beatles Buffet.' The gigs and the radio show are fun, but there is still something missing," he told her as he leaned in, looking her in the eyes.

"What is that, Johnny Moondog?" Jody grinned as she

251

spoke. Her face flushed and her eyes glistened.

"Well, I, ah, well I would, ah...."

"Spit it out, John!"

"I want to spend a lot more time with you. The police force absorbed most of my time, but I am ready to move ahead, and actually have a relationship that isn't with a psychotic killer. I would like for us to hang out together more," he blurted, but afterward felt more like he had blundered.

"Are you saying that you would like us to be in a committed relationship?" she teased.

"Yeah, that's it. I really like you, and I can't wait to be with you. I guess what I'm asking is if we can go steady? I even brought my class ring along, just in case you said yes," he said with a big grin. Jody liked his sometimes innocent charm. Her smile showed that she was very interested in his proposal.

"Johnny Moondog, will you ever mature?" she said while rolling her eyes.

"Probably not," he shrugged with his answer.

"Good," she exclaimed. "Now, where's that ring?" Her fingers waved a give-it-to-me gesture.

They were still laughing as the waitress brought their salads.

The meal was excellent, and Jody popped her head into the kitchen to tell Chef Robert how much they'd enjoyed it. When she sat back down, she and John continued to giggle, even when his phone rang. He had quit jumping each time the phone rang. He had quit expecting Bungalow Bill's psychotic clues. He was still smiling when he hit the talk button.

From the speaker floated, "You know, if you break my heart I'll go, But I'll be back again

'Cause I told you once before goodbye, But I came back

again."

He looked up. His face was sullen. Any smile or joy he had felt for the last few hours was gone. Watson pulled in a long, hard breath and blew out a long sigh. He said with great disappointment, "It's the Beatles 'I'll Be Back.'"

About the Author

Timothy W. Ayers is the author of *The Sign of the End* and several best-selling children's books. He received an Award for the Best Speculative Fiction for 2017 for his book, *Cruel Messenger*. Tim lives along the Mississippi River in an attempt to channel his inner-Mark Twain. When Tim is not turning out historical fiction alongside his co-author and grandson, Jude B. Rennie, he is plotting his next action thrillers.

www.ingramcontent.com/pod-product-compliance
Lightning Source LLC
Chambersburg PA
CBHW022002170626
46808CB00001B/254